The Intimate Memoir of
Dame Jenny Everleigh

Book Two: An age of pleasure

In which, for the licentious Jenny, Britain comes first!

The Intimate Memoir
of
Dame Jenny Everleigh

Book Two: An Age of Pleasure

Sphere Books Limited

First published in the United States of America by Pocket Books, 1986
Copyright © 1986 by Jerry Yulsman
Published by Sphere Books Ltd, 1987
27 Wrights Lane, London W8 5TZ

TRADE
MARK

Set in 10/11 Sabon

Printed and bound in Great Britain by
Cox & Wyman Ltd, Reading

*Being the personal recollections of one Jenny Everleigh
and her life of devotion to Queen, Country and Pleasure
amongst the gentlemen and the fools of Merry England
and the heroes, rogues and the wogs of its Empire, on
which the sun has never yet set, nor shall it.*

Prologue

The young girl I had once been still resides in this antique hulk. If given the privilege to live it all again, she would change nothing, not a single adventure; neither action nor spoken word. Ah, how sweet it was! How marvellous to be sought after, to be fashionable; to be a cultured and glamorous figure of the demimonde known for her beuty, her charm, her wit. (Surely at this stage I can be forgiven a certain lack of modesty.) And how satisfying to know that I stood at what was then the centre of the universe —Britannia at the height of her glory! I had within me the seeds of greatness, deposited at one time or another into an hospitable quim that played hostess to the most imposing pricks of an exciting, but piquantly innocent time.

I recall observing a seventeenth birthday in my father's humble blacksmith shop in Liverpool. Just a short time later, as those things go, I was celebrating my eighteenth in a London whorehouse of quality and repute. Following that, I retain a pleasurable memory of my nineteenth being toasted by a naked prince: Tewfik Pasha, a future khedive of Egypt. Then the dawn of my twentieth year found me in the appreciative arms of yet another prince: the future King of England. In short, I had risen quickly and steadily in the world. In just two years and a few months after setting foot, penniless and innocent, onto the sainted pavement of the greatest of cities, I found myself (through diligent effort) in possession of an upper-class accent, a deposit in Barclay's (twelve thousand pounds sterling), and a knighthood in the French Legion of Honour.

(If indeed, I have aroused the curiosity of those readers who have not yet read my initial memoir, allow me, with all due modesty, to recommend that earlier tome.)

—Dame Jenny Everleigh, Côte d'Azur, 1920.

We begin in the year 1871,
the 12,356th day of Victoria's reign

ONE

For a man to be a great lover he must first appreciate, respect and, above all, crave the social and intellectual company of women. Allow me to add that the reverse is also true. [H.G. Wells]

The future king of England flicked a flaccid member, still dampened with my love-syrup, in order to expose the underside to cooling breezes from my bedroom window. 'In a short time,' said he, 'twill be your birthday.' He reached over to the side table to consult his pocket watch and to retrieve a small, elongated box. 'In just one minute and thirty seconds, to be exact.' With a flourishing show of ceremony, he placed it in my hands.

'*Pour moi?*'

'Of course. But you are not to open it till I give the word.'

It was a lovely box; beribboned, wrapped in violet paper. Its shape left me with little doubt that my gift was to be a necklace; but a necklace of what? Diamonds or pearls? Impatient, I glanced down at my supine lover with the irrational hope that I might find the answer there. Edward's eyes strayed for a moment from the face of his watch to mine. 'Fifty-seven seconds,' said he, his expression a mask of mock severity. 'The hour of midnight approaches . . .'

With his gift cradled in my hands, I hovered, naked, above him, straddling his body as, intently, he counted the seconds. How boyish he seemed, how sweet. My venal

1

conjecture dissolved in a sudden flush of guilt and affection. 'Tis not, thought I, pearls or diamonds but truly the thought that counts. Starting now, I vowed, I must strive more diligently for moral perfection.

Seated patiently on his chest, with my moist scented garden just inches from his face, I sighed with the memory of our other pleasurable encounters. There had been a varied succession of beds. The first of these had been a modest cot in the London home of yet another friend: the painter, James McNeill Whistler. Later, I frolicked with my royal lover on a canopied monstrosity in the khedive's palace in Cairo. Then shortly after that, we had shared a silken nest aboard the *Aigle:* the royal yacht of France. (Yes, my dear reader, the insidious rumours were correct; Empress Eugénie *was* in it at the time.) But now I was entertaining my prince in my very own bed, in my very own flat! How cosy, how intimate it seemed. I had truly arrived!

'Time,' said Edward.

With an unsuccessful attempt at ladylike fastidiousness, I ripped the wrapping from the box. Then, taking a deep breath and closing my eyes, I opened it.

'Happy birthday . . . Jenny.'

My guess had been somewhat off the mark. 'Twas indeed a necklace, but neither pearls nor diamonds. I opened my eyes on rubies! Strung with pure gold, the stones gleamed blood red on their bed of soft black silk. I stared, speechless. It was a birthday gift worthy of a princess!

'Allow me,' said Edward.

As I watched, boggle-eyed, he removed the necklace from its box and, reaching up, draped it about my neck. I leaned forward, bending my head as he manipulated the clasp.

'Beautiful.'

In the mirror, at the head of the bed, a fortune in red rubies punctuated the soft swell of my breasts. 'It leaves me breathless . . . it is gorgeous!'

'It would not be nearly so on any other woman.'

'Oh, Edward thank you . . . I can't imagine what else I can say . . .'

'Say nothing, Jenny. A kiss is all I ask.'

'Oh Edward . . .' As I bent down to comply he placed his hands on my hips.

'No, my dear,' said he, his voice soft, the eyes that gazed into mine even softer and filled with desire. 'There are other lips I crave more.'

'Anything,' said I.

His hands slipped down to grasp the yielding flesh of my buttocks. Seated as I was on his abdomen, it was a simple matter for him to pull me forward till I squatted high on his chest.

'Kiss me.'

'Yes,' I whispered, inching forward till I straddled his face.

'Spread your lips for me, dear lady.'

My fingers sought my gorged labia. I pulled gently, looking down to view the blooming of an exotic pink flower damp with the dew of passion and the copious pearls of my lover's recent spending. Edward followed my glance. His tongue emerged like the head of an inquisitive snake.

'There my darling,' said I, softly. ''Tis open for you. Kiss me, kiss my cunt.' I brought my pussy to his mouth as if offering him a kiss on more conventional lips.

His mouth opened to the soft, yielding flesh, his tongue probing gently into the portal. I closed my eyes, throwing my head back to luxuriate in a tingling that suffused my nether region. A deep groan formed in my throat as his tongue, sure of itself now, penetrated, then fluttered about inside me.

'Ah, Edward you're so good to me!'

He tongued lightly, teasingly, lapping his way upward. I quivered in expectation, my fingers pulling gently, stretching the fervent flesh even more, opening the flower to my

3

lover's passionate laving. His tongue made tentative contact with the very tip of my clitoris, causing an exquisite prickling to spread from its source to my breasts, the back of my neck, the base of my spine.

'Lovely,' said my prince, muttering, almost incoherently, into a gushing quim. 'Tell me my sweet . . . tell me . . .'

''Tis heaven,' I sighed. 'Exquisite . . . You are a champion, dear Edward . . . yes, like that! I feel I will melt.'

He tweaked firmly now, transmitting tactile shocks to the erected, supersensitive love-arrow. I reached down to grasp his head, locking it in place as my arse rotated with insistent rhythm – pressing, rubbing my swollen cunt against his mouth. In response, he squeezed my bottom cheeks even tighter, pulling me closer till I thought I would surely smother him in oozing pussy flesh! My moans were a low-pitched tremolo, continuous now; controlled counterpoint to the rapturous trembling of my body.

I was halfway up the mountain. The peak was in clear view! My clitoris was between his lips, suctioned into his mouth; the subject of a tempestuous tongue lashing! I rode his face with the gyrating hips of a dervish. I was being ravished! Eaten alive!

'Heaven!' I shouted, my entire body jerking spasmodically. 'I'm going to spend! Suck! Suck me!'

I held his head more tightly as he moved downward, his nose pressed against my spasming love-button as he fucked me now, with a stiffened tongue!

'Ah, you devil,' said I breathlessly. 'You love doing it . . . you love my cunt.'

'Yesss!' said he, in muffled voice. 'I love it! Ah, Jenny, your sweet cunt! Succulent! Drown me in it! Fuck my face!'

Bursting into a series of uncontrolled twitchings, tremblings, spasms, I called out, 'I'm cumming, Edward! I'm spending for you! There! Drink it! Suck it out of me . . . it's all yours . . . everything!'

Moments later I lay next to him. His face, his beard were sopping with my juices. I kissed him, at first affectionately, then, as I tasted my essence on his lips, passionately.

'Happy birthday, darling,' said he as I released him in order that we both might breathe.

'Thank you Edward, dearest. You have made it the best of all my birthdays.'

'And the day just begins.'

I ran my fingertips across his chest, then slowly down the length of his body. His pego remained limp, soft and friendly to my touch. I traced the underside of its bulbous head with a delicate finger. Slowly it began to stiffen.

'Jenny . . .'

'Yes?'

'I must speak with you.'

'Speak, my prince.' The fingers of my other hand caressed the secret place just beneath his buttocks.

'I find it difficult to concentrate while you . . .'

'Ah, then 'tis serious talk you have in mind?'

'Quite.'

His prick was approaching its full extension. I grasped it, pumped delicately. 'Then it will have to wait,' said I, trailing kisses down the length of his body. 'I have much more important business to attend to.'

'Jenny . . .'

His member was a royal monument towering above the wild, hairy forest at its base. I ran a tentative tongue about its head. Britain was well represented by this imperial sceptre. It was a weapon of modest, though respectable dimension, forged of honest British steel. Edward always wielded it forthrightly; this particular prince was the embodiment of the empire over which he would eventually rule. He possessed charm, wit, and a commanding presence; he was a good fellow, loyal to his friends, but sadly unimaginative. Like his country, perfection eluded him. 'S truth. This left him hardly the greatest of lovers. (But no matter, I possessed sufficient imagination for the two of us.) Nevertheless, credit where it was due: Edward was indeed enamoured of women. He was a true gentleman and dedicated student of the intricate science of female pleasure. As history was to tell us, this Prince of Wales was sincere. So suffice it to say that our lovemaking, though it lacked a certain exotic quality, nevertheless constituted a series of vigorous, though tender unions.

I sucked happily on his prick, losing myself in that delightful labour of love. It is an activity to which I am dedicated and for which I show a natural talent.

'Jenny, I must speak with you,' said Edward. The words were paced far apart, his voice strained.

'I'm sorry, Your Royal Highness,' said I with mock seriousness, 'but I've been taught that a lady should never speak with her mouth full.' With that, I engulfed his stiffened pego to half its length.

He sat up, dislodging me from love's labour. 'Jenny,' said he, 'I assume you to be a most loyal subject of England and of your sovereign.'

'Of course, Edward dear,' said I, with an awakening awareness that he was, indeed, serious. 'Surely I haven't given you reason to assume otherwise.' Wondering at what he was getting, I, once again, laid hold of his prick.

Gently, he brushed my hand away. 'I must speak of this matter whilst I still have the wit to do so.'

'But there is a time and place for everything, dearest.'

'Then, darling Jenny, this will be both time and place.'

Defeated, I sat up next to him, my back against the headboard, my hands folded demurely in my lap like a schoolgirl (albeit naked) awaiting her lesson. 'All right, Edward,' said I petulantly. 'What is this in aid of?'

He sighed, as if in relief, then after a moment's pause, said, 'An affair of state, dear lady.'

'Of state?'

'Yes.' He turned to me. 'Brittania approaches a crisis and has need of your services.'

'Britannia?' I was dazed by his words. What had promised

6

to be a night of lust – of love – had suddenly turned into something else. What?

'Of all the people in Great Britain, you seem to be the most qualified to deal with this matter.' He looked into my eyes. ''Tis a mission of great importance, you see, and . . .' He grasped my hand, squeezed it. 'A mission that might indeed, prove to be of considerable danger.'

'To me?'

'Yes, if, indeed, you agree to undertake it.' His eyes burned into mine, their intensity validating the seriousness of his discourse.

I had never seen Edward thus. A momentary nervousness gripped my loins. 'I know nothing of affairs of state,' said I in a small voice. 'Surely you flatter me. I mean . . . as a mere girl, what could I possibly do?'

'A mere girl, Jenny? The female device of false modesty will get you nowhere with me.' He was out of bed, pacing to the end of the room and back. Finally, he stood at the foot, towering over me. 'The affair at Suez, last year, proved your courage to be the equal of any man in the empire! You are the first British woman to be a chevalier of the French Legion of Honour – no – the first woman of any nationality to receive that honour. How proud I was to be an Englishman that morning on the *Aigle*, when the Empress Eugénie bestowed it on you.'

Embarrassed by his tribute, I said, quietly. 'Tell me what I must do, Edward . . . and why.'

'First, you must seduce a man named Harry Fibbit – Sir Harry, to be exact.'

'Yes?'

'Intimacy is the road to confidence. He must learn to trust you. We need certain information.'

'You mean, I'm to become his mistress?'

'In a manner of speaking, yes.'

'Why do you say, "in a manner of speaking"?'

'He has many mistresses.' Edward crossed the room, retrieved a cigar from his waistcoat. 'May I?'

7

'Please do.'

Using a silver tool, he clipped the end, then lit up. 'Sir Harry Fibbit is a traitor to the Crown. He is in league with the Turks and their master, in a plot to turn the Suez Canal into an Ottoman and Prussian waterway.'

'Shouldn't that be an affair for the French? It is their canal.'

'Perhaps, but the French will soon be occupied in a war with the Prussians. It is a war that will tax all their strength and one they may very well lose. No, dear Jenny, if the Suez Canal is to be defended, then we ourselves must do it. It must remain open to us. Along with Gibraltar it controls the portals to our empire. Britain cannot afford it to fall into the hands of potential enemies. If that happened, our major trade route to India would once again be routed the long way, around the horn of Africa . . . unthinkable.'

'But the canal is on Turkish territory,' said I, brashly. 'Egypt is part of the Turkish – the Ottoman – Empire.'

'The Suez Canal is an essential part of our British destiny. Britain looks to the new century, the Turks look back on the last. The Ottoman Empire rots in the sun. Actually, Egypt is virtually independent. Thirty-seven per cent of the Suez Company shares are owned personally by the khedive of Egypt.'

'And Sir Harry Fibbit?'

Edward's voice was projected from a dense cloud of blue tobacco smoke that all but obscured its source. 'He is a despicable man who is betraying his country. The French, because of the threat of war, need money. Sir Harry is buying Suez Canal shares from them for his secret Turkish and Prussian masters.'

'Why can't the Turks buy their shares directly?'

'France would not sell to them, nor will they sell to us. Only the Dutch, the Swedes, the Swiss, and the Americans are eligible, and only a specific amount is available. Sir Harry has organized a sham corporation based in Zurich and another, just as bogus, in Philadelphia in the

Commonwealth of Pennsylvania. After they have purchased the outstanding shares, the villains intend to convince the khedive, Said Pasha, to sell them his. 'Twill be a simple matter as the Egyptian economy is debt-ridden. That will make the Turkish-Prussian consortium majority stockholder. Then, with the French preoccupied in their Prussian war, they will assume sole ownership. Turks and Prussians will take control; they will station troops to protect their investment. We must prevent that from happening.'

There was something not quite right about Edward's explanation. Quietly I said, 'Why not simply inform the French of Harry Fibbit's underhanded dealings?'

'Ah, you are a sharp lass, to be sure.' He paused, grinning at me as if somehow I had found him out. 'The truth is that we want not merely to stop the Turks and Prussians in their tracks, but for the good of the empire the canal must be secure; under our control. The French wouldn't care for that either, though I dare say they'd prefer us to their enemy, the Hun.'

'But the khedive, Said Pasha . . .'

'If he refuses to sell to us, then his son most certainly will.'

'I see,' said I, recalling young Tewfik's passion for all things British. Quietly I said, 'He will replace his father on the throne.'

'We will see to that.'

'And in the bargain,' said I, 'Egypt will become part of the empire and we will control both entrance *and* exit to the Mediterranean. It will become a British lake. What you speak of as an "affair of state" is more a matter of imperial expansion.'

'Precisely.' He loomed over me. 'The Suez Canal simply cannot be entrusted to anyone else. And we, not the French or the Turks, must control Egypt: can't have one without the other.' He paused, stared into my eyes. 'Are you with us?'

'Of course, Your Royal Highness.'

9

'Ah, I knew you would be.'

'What am I to do?'

'You must befriend Sir Harry Fibbit, become a member of his household, and report everything you see and hear that might be relevant. We must know what he is up to, and even more important, we must prevent the shares he is purchasing from getting into Turkish hands. They will not purchase the khedive's portion until then.' Once again, Edward delved into the pockets of his waistcoat. He handed me a ragged-edged paper. It had been torn from the London *Times*. An advertisement atop the second column, read: EDITOR-LIBRARIAN WANTED TO PREPARE GENTLEMAN'S MEMOIRS FOR PUBLICATION. A box number followed.

TWO

A woman lives three quarters of her life with the memory of the fleeting beauty of the other quarter. How sad.
[Victor Hugo]

It was just past noon under thickening clouds as I, the only passenger to do so, debarked at the small station at Driffield, a quiet Yorkshire village on the edge of Marston Moor. Within my view, the sole sign of life was an elderly man seated atop a pony trap. But was he indeed a sign of life? He slouched, his chin resting on a chest that seemed unaminated by mortal breath.

'Sir . . .' The word accomplished little more than to awaken the pony who swung his head about to glare at me. Undaunted, I repeated the call, which elicited only an angry equine whinny loud enough to awaken any but the dead. The decrepit driver remained unmoved. I reached up, grasped his sleeve, and jerked. 'Sir . . .'

This time 'twas a human eye that cocked open to glare at me. 'Are you for hire?' said I, relieved at the old man's return from what I feared might have been more congenial climes.

The baleful grey eye finally blinked as the other opened. The elderly driver cleared his throat and in barely discernible English, said, 'Fanshawe House?'

'Yes.'

'Ah then, are you the one I've been sent to fetch?'

'Miss Jenny Everleigh is my name.'

11

'Then you'd be the one.' He reached down for my travelling case. I boarded the small, two-wheeled cart from the rear and we were off.

Once through the village, the road degenerated into little more than a rutted track wandering through the barren, low-lying hills. Under a darkening sky, the dismal landscape was rendered in shades of grey — colourless, lifeless. I hummed a little tune to cheer myself.

Before we had gone a mile, the driver, his head lolling from side to side, was once again in the arms of Morpheus. His resonant snores were measured accompaniment to the rhythmic squealing of the wheels, the melancholy whispering of a chilling wind. I raised my collar, huddling deeper into the warmth of the ill-chosen, light coat I thought would be more than adequate for May. The road, as viewed from a slight rise, had evolved into a wavering line stretching to a grim horizon, its length unpunctuated by any sign of human habitation. Our destination was nowhere in sight. The pony, given his head, plodded on. The grey sky was turning blue.

Well over two hours had passed when the sun emerged. In the distance I perceived a house marked by a beacon of chimney smoke spiralling skyward. As we grew closer, it evolved into a stately, Georgian mansion of considerable size, squatting forthrightly on a sward of green through which ran a small brook. A parklike outpost in a bleak wasteland, its large radius was defined by ancient oaks and elms.

As we drew closer, I once again read the letter I had received in answer to my reply to the ad in *The Times*. It was written in precise, heavy black chancery script: *If you will be good enough to come up to Fanshawe House on Tuesday next, the undersigned will be pleased to discuss the possibility of your future employment. From Kings Cross there is a 7:25 to Newcastle. The train stops at Driffield when requested. You will be met at the station. Your ticket is enclosed. We look forward to meeting you . . .*

I felt a pang of trepidation. I had never played a role

before. Could I sustain such playacting? Could I indeed fulfil the function of a secretary, an editor? What kind of man was Sir Harry Fibbit?

The pony made its way down a gracefully curved cobblestone driveway lined with elms. It stopped just a few yards from the squat, stone facade. Above the massive doorway, carved into the ornate lintel were the words: FANSHAWE HOUSE. The driver slept on as I disembarked.

Fanshawe House was a dignified old lady dressed in handsome, moneyed grey, her jewellery gleaming with the burnished well-worn patina of polished brass. A small name plate at the entrance read FIBBIT. I tugged twice on the bell pull to be rewarded by the sound of an inside door being opened. Moments later I was facing a tall, blond man in the entranceway. He towered over me, a Norse god dressed incongruously in butler's livery.

'May I help you, madam?' His voice, despite the sparse phrase it enunciated, was singularly unbutlerlike, melodious: beneath it lurked a deep, menacing undertone.

'I'm here,' said I, concealing my nervousness, 'in response to the advertisement in *The Times*: my name is Jenny Everleigh.'

The butler's eyes took me in with one gulp like a snake consuming its prey. 'Please come in.'

He took my brolly and travel case and escorted me into a small entrance hall. I found his gaunt face and piercing eyes oddly disconcerting. 'Will Madam have a seat?' His gaze descended brazenly down the length of my body. I found myself doing likewise, starting at his shoulders, surveying his long, thin frame. The parting of his morning coat revealed and emphasized a large, bulbous lump canted to the left of centre inside his trouser leg. It amused me to contemplate the fact that most Englishmen dressed on the right; this young and insolent butler was obviously a noncomformist. I wondered briefly if he expressed the same kind of individuality when he put the thing to use.

I raised my eyes to find his awaiting me. Then, to my

13

astonishment, he placed his hand firmly on the bulge of his crotch and squeezed!

'I'll inform Lady Fibbit of your presence.' He turned quickly and exited, leaving me with a fleeting, but nevertheless graphic impression of a delightfully insolent little arse. 'Twas indeed an intriguing introduction to what I suspected would be a most interesting household!

Less than a minute later, I felt a presence behind me. 'Good morning, Miss Everleigh, I am Lady Doris Fibbit.' She had entered behind me through another door. She was a tall graceful woman of indeterminate age. Her features were feline with large, radiant, round-brown eyes framed by the curving arc of precise eyebrows. I was startled to find that they were drawn or painted onto her skin; those provided by nature having been either shaved or plucked! Was this some newfangled fashion of which I was unaware?

'I'm pleased to meet you,' said I, with a small curtsey.

Lady Fibbit smiled, revealing two rows of perfect, pearl-white teeth — much too perfect actually, for any but the youngest Englishwoman. 'Delighted,' said she, extending her hand. Her fingernails were inordinately long, painted bright red, and pointed like sharpened cat's claws! Perhaps here was yet another novel fashion of which I was ignorant.

Fumbling about in my purse, I said, 'I received a reply . . . ah, here it is.' I handed her the letter.

Lady Fibbit shook her head. 'That won't be necessary, my dear. As the letter states, we've been expecting you. 'And I must apologize for the pony cart. Our coachman has been taken with a spot of ague and we were obliged to make do with the gardener. I pray it was not too arduous.'

'Not at all.'

She took my hand and once again I was being surveyed from head to toe. 'Lovely,' said she, through lips reddened with rouge. 'Most charming. My husband will be quite pleased with you.'

14

'Thank you,' said I, somewhat lamely. She seemed a strange woman.

'May I call you Jenny?'

'Yes, do.'

'Jenny: such a lively name. We must have tea and a chat. Sir Harry will be home presently and in the meanwhile you can tell me all about yourself.'

With my hand still in hers she led me through the house to a large sunny room furnished entirely in white rattan. 'Here we are, dear Jenny,' she said, as we seated ourselves at a small round marble table. A modest formal garden glowed in the afternoon sun through a row of French doors. 'I just adore this room when the sun is shining. Unfortunately in London, it seems to shine less and less these days. Don't you agree?'

'I believe so.'

''Tis a most disconcerting phenomenon.'

'Most disconcerting,' said I, in agreement.

'Sir Harry says it is the price we must pay for the amenities of modern civilization.'

'Civilization?'

'The burning of coal, my dear; he insists that is is changing the climate.'

'How awful,' said I, gazing into the garden and wondering if perhaps it were true. I turned to find Lady Doris staring at my bosom.

'Lovely,' said she, reaching out to pull a convenient bell rope. She rose from her chair. 'I think it would be quite nice to open a window or two.' I watched her as she glided across the room. 'I simply adore air, don't you?'

'I find it most essential,' said I, beginning to suspect Lady Fibbit to be quite eccentric, perhaps a little mad (but charming nonetheless). I stared unabashed, admiring her erect posture, her curvaceous figure so well delineated in the silk dressing gown. She possessed a kind of ageless poise. Yet there was something decidedly wrong. I found myself wondering as to her age. The answer, when it struck was an aberrant one, an impression born of neither logic nor instinct: the fleeting, inexplicable vision of an ancient harridan encased in the body of a young woman!

She turned, catching me out. 'Not so terrible for an old hag, eh?'

'Sorry, I didn't mean to stare.' Had she been reading my mind?

'Yes, you did, you meant to stare and I'm flattered.' She opened a pair of double French doors. 'Ah, that's lovely . . . fresh country air.' She stretched then sniffed the air as one might sample a fish.

'Delightful,' said I.

Lady Doris returned to the table, hips swaying. 'You find me attractive?'

'Indeed, yes,' said I emphatically. I'd play her game.

'Do you think you could guess my age?'

'I wouldn't dare.'

'Try, I'm quite curious.'

'Must I?'

'Please.'

'Well, it presents a problem.'

'Problem?' said she, smiling knowingly. 'What problem, my dear?'

'Should I deal with what seems to be your physical age – your apparent age – or what I sense, rather strangely, to be your actual age?'

The smile faded from Lady Doris's face to be quickly replaced by another, less sincere. 'Whichever you prefer.' Her voice was suddenly low.

'Well, your physical age, in terms of your appearance, I would place at about thirty or so.'

'How sweet you are, dear Jenny, and how perceptive.' She reached across the table to squeeze my hand. 'And?'

'Your actual age?'

'Yes.'

'It would be most difficult to estimate.' Forty came to mind but this was a very strange game indeed and I felt

16

suddenly reticent. What if it were a wrong guess and she was only thirty-five?

'Try.'

'Madam, you are ageless,' said I, 'so it matters not.' Despite the platitude, my curiosity was growing.

Her face lit up. 'Most profound, young Jenny! Precisely the way I prefer to think of myself.' She leaned forward, brought my hand to her open bodice, guiding it inside. 'Here, dear child, feel this.'

My hand was on her naked breast! Astounded. I found myself cupping it, squeezing: it was firm, beautifully sculpted. Quietly, I said. ''Tis the breast of a young girl of eighteen.'

'Indeed it is.' Lady Fibbit pressed my hand with hers. I felt the fat protuberance of an erect nipple insinuate itself between my fingers. 'And the rest of my body also. Only my face begins to show age.'

'Amazing.'

'The other,' she said proudly, 'is its equal.'

'Beautiful.'

'You may keep your hand there, Jenny, it feels quite nice.' She closed her eyes, licked her lips, and sighed. 'A woman's greatest asset is her beauty. One must do all one can to retain it for as long as possible, don't you agree?'

'It is our duty as women,' said I, tracing her aureole with a gentle fingertip even as my curiosity grew.

'Unfortunately, few women of our time retain their natural beauty beyond the age of – say – thirty-five, and none beyond forty.'

In a quiet voice, I said, 'And you, Lady Doris?'

She laughed. 'Since you refused to conjecture, you must promise to believe me.'

'Done.'

'I was born during the reign of King George the Third.'

'Good Lord!'

'The year was 1816.'

''Twas three monarchs ago! Astonished, I did some quick mental arithmetic. 'You are fifty-five years old!'

'Precisely.'

''Tis almost impossible to believe!'

'You promised you would.'

'Surely you practise sorcery.'

'Precisely, my dear, sorcery it is; but not witchcraft, if that's what you're thinking.'

'Then how . . .?'

'Ah, that is my secret.' She opened her eyes. 'But perhaps I might share it with you. Then you too can retain your beauty long after your peers have lost theirs. I'm sure you'd find that a most delightful prospect. You seem a worthy young woman with a beauty deserving of preservation.'

'I would be most appreciative.' I tweaked her nipple as my curiosity grew. Was she possessed of some sort of magic potion? A secret fountain of youth, right here in England?

Our discussion was interrupted by a rhythmic squeaking. I removed my hand from Lady Doris's lovely, pneumatic breast, then turned to find the sound coming from the wheels of a tea cart propelled by a very beautiful girl.

'Tea, mum.'

'Thank you, Bettina,' said Lady Fibbit. 'I forgot I had ordered it.'

'Yes, mum.' She wore a starched white shirtwaist, a white apron, and long grey skirt. I guessed her age to be fifteen. She was quite blond, with a face that exhibited both the complexion and the unblinking, inexpressiveness of a precious porcelain doll. I found it difficult to take my eyes from her as she wheeled the cart to the table and proceeded to lay out the tea things: sliced carrots, apple wedges, and such like; strange fare, more suitable, thought I, for a rabbit hutch than for a civilized, afternoon tea.

'Bettina is a little minx,' said Lady Doris. 'Aren't you Bettina?'

'Yes mum.'

As the delightful servant girl bent at the waist to lay out the tea things, I glanced into an ornately carved cheval mirror across the room. A rear view greeted my eye. Her skirt, obviously slit to the waist, had opened, exposing her naked arse!

'This is Miss Jenny Everleigh, Bettina,' said Lady Doris. 'She will be living with us for a while.'

'Yes, mum. Pleased, I'm sure.' The young servant girl curtsied prettily, causing the skirt to close.

'You are to treat Miss Everleigh as one of the family.'

'Yes, mum.'

'Thank you, Bettina,' said I, smiling at her, then glancing out of the corner of my eye into the mirror. Again, the slit, like a theatrical curtain, had parted to reveal the delightful pink rotundities. Even as I watched, I could see Lady Fibbit's hand curl snakelike around the fleshy buttocks reaching down between them into the soft juncture of Bettina's naked thighs.

'Sugar?' said Lady Fibbit.

'Yes, please,' said I, feeling my cheeks flush with what I assumed was the same shade of pink as Bettina's nether ones. 'Twas indeed an eccentric household. What further oddities awaited me? In the glass, the maid spread her legs, providing the older woman easier access.

'One lump or two?'

'Lump?' I asked, preoccupied with the astonishing sight in the looking-glass.

'Sugar, Miss Everleigh?'

'Ah, one please.'

Using a pair of silver tongs in her right hand, Lady Doris served the sugar whilst her left busied herself in a more secret and lascivious pursuit. Framed in the guilding of the graceful mirror, it was obvious, that the older woman was frigging the young girl! Her thumb, braced against a smooth rounded arsecheek was acting as a fulcrum for busy, stroking fingers.

Lady Doris caught my eye, following it to the mirror.

She turned back to smile at me, knowingly. 'I hope,' said she, 'you don't disapprove of our little diversion.'

'Not at all,' said I.

'Then I'm quite pleased with you and I'm sure that Sir Harry will also be.' She slapped the little maid playfully on her bottom. 'All right, Bettina.'

'Will that be all, mum?'

'Yes, for now, child. I'll ring if I need you, and tell Starns to inform Sir Harry, when he arrives, that we're in the morning room.' She poured the tea as I watched Bettina's exit in the mirror, her skirt appearing like any other, with no hint of its naughty slit.

I said. 'I'm beginning to feel like Alice.'

'Alice?'

'*Through the Looking-Glass.*'

'Really?'

'I've been here only twenty minutes,' said I vaguely. The tea seemed strange, though not unpleasantly so.

'Would you care for a carrot?' said the Queen of Hearts.

THREE

Take heed, do not confuse love with need. [Bertram Trasker]

Sir Harry Fibbit seemed hardly the villainous traitor I had been led to expect. He was a large, jovial man in his fifties. We spoke for a few minutes about my qualifications for secretarial employment. He seemed pleased with me; I was equally pleased with him. 'Twas all quite pleasant and friendly and I had to remind myself that the actual, secret purpose for my presence in this mad household was to spy for Her Majesty's government.

Starns, the tall, blond butler entered, bearing a tray of refreshments. He seemed no less diabolic than when I had first viewed him. For just a moment, he stared blankly into my eyes, then in his earlier, insolent manner, surveyed my full length, from head to toe. As he placed the tray on a serving table and turned to leave the room I once again found myself fascinated by a delightful, well-rounded arse emphasized graphically by outrageously tight trousers.

'Miss Everleigh,' said Sir Harry. 'Do you prefer your libation from Spain or Scotland?'

'I fear,' said I, aware of a strange tingling in my loins, ''tis a bit early in the day for either, thank you.' I sipped what remained of my tea.

'Sherry *pour moi*,' said Lady Doris.

Sir Harry poured whisky and soda for himself, sherry for Lady Doris. 'Have you met any of our household yet, Miss Everleigh?'

'The butler and the maid,' said I.

'Ahh, Bettina,' said he. 'She's a charming little thing, don't you agree?'

'Charming,' said I.

'Miss Everleigh has equated us with Alice's wonderland,' said Lady Doris.

'Oh really? You find us eccentric?'

'Frankly yes . . . but then, there are those who consider me likewise.' I was feeling suddenly light-headed; strangely gay, as if I had been sipping the sherry or whisky I'd so recently refused.

'Well, by George,' said Sir Harry Fibbit, his tone jovial. 'I suppose we are a bit eccentric.' He laughed. 'But I am happy to hear that you are too. Birds of a feather, eh?'

'Ah, Noel dear,' said Lady Doris. I turned to see a young man enter the room. He looked no more than nineteen or twenty and was wearing a blue blazer with white trousers — a very handsome young man.

'Good morning, Mother, Father,' he said in a clipped Oxford accent.

'I thought,' said Lady Doris, 'that you were in Edinburgh seeing that young lady . . . what'sername.'

'I was, Mother, yesterday. Her name is Deborah MacDill.'

'I'm sure she's quite charming,' said Lady Doris, sipping on her sherry. 'Have you fucked her yet?'

'Not yet, Mother.'

'Time waits for no man, son,' said Sir Harry.

'I understand, Father, but she has a most stubborn propensity for chastity.'

Lady Doris, turning to her husband, placed a protective hand on her son's arm. 'I'm certain Noel is doing his best, Harry.'

'He may have to do even better than that,' said the master of the household. 'One does not go about saying he's going to do something and then simply not do it unless one is a liar, a ponce, or a Frenchman.'

'Yes, Father.'

'When a man makes a commitment, he must see it through, come hell or high water. It matters not whether the object is to take a hill from the enemy or to deflower a virgin.'

'Yes, Father.'

'Then get on with it, my boy.'

For some reason, I was neither shocked nor surprised by what was, indeed, a most unconventional family exchange. I smiled vaguely at the young man, my brain feeling as if it were weirdly swathed in cotton batting.

'My-my, we're neglecting our guest,' said Lady Doris. She introduced me. Once again I was under intense inspection. Noel Fibbit, like his parents, made no attempt at subtlety. It was as if he were seeing through my clothes. I was quite suddenly preoccupied with a strange tingling sensation in my groin. As the young Fibbit took my hand, the somewhat pleasant sensation seemed to blossom into an uncomfortable itch.

'I look forward to seeing more of you,' he said, with an engaging smile.

'Plenty of time for that, Noel, my boy,' said Sir Harry. 'First things first, as we say. You've still the virgin MacDill to conquer. 'There'll be no other girls for you till you honour that commitment.'

'Not even Bettina?'

'None.'

'Yes, Father.'

I found their conversation peculiarly engaging despite the fact that for some reason my head seemed to be spinning. It was not an unpleasant sensation. But how had I managed to get *tipsy* on nothing more than a cup of tea? As the boy left the room, there were *ta-ta's* all round. I shivered, fighting an almost uncontrollable desire to rub my quim.

'Good lad, that,' said Sir Harry. 'We're going to make a man of him, but first, he must learn some discipline.'

23

'Ah, Harry, you've always been too hard on him,' said Lady Doris.

The two seemed to be wavering — shimmering — before my eyes as if I were viewing them through imperfect glass. I found it difficult to maintain a dignified seating posture, fighting, as best I could, against a tendency to slump in my chair.

'Are you comfortable, Miss Everleigh?' Sir Harry's voice seemed to come from a far distance.

'I'm not quite sure.' A vagueness now permeated my being, making coherent thought difficult.

'Perhaps you might prefer to stretch out on the settee,' said Lady Doris, her voice pitched in kindly tones.

'Perhaps . . .' To no avail. I made a valiant effort to retain, at least a shred of dignity. I had lost control of my face. It seemed to be melting.

Each of them took an arm, supporting me as if I were a full-sized rag doll. 'I've gone India Rubber all over,' said I, in a small, barely audible voice.

'Lovely,' said Sir Harry.

'Lovely,' I repeated vaguely, as they stretched me out on the settee. I was afloat in a delicious sea of languor. It was all quite wonderful except for the pickling itch, that seemed now, to have buried itself deep in my vagina. I realized that rubbing or scratching would be to little avail. Something more was needed.

'Ah, she is beautiful,' said Sir Harry. 'I must see the rest of her.'

'You shall,' said Lady Doris.

Though the import of their words seemed clouded, I realized dimly, they were speaking of me. I squirmed about under the influence of a strange and increasing randyness.

'She seems ready, my dear.'

'Yes, she's quite ripe,' said Lady Doris. Then, with her smiling face just inches from mine, she said, 'How do you feel, dearest Jenny?'

'Wonderful,' said I, hearing my own voice as though from a distance. 'But there is a most diabolical itching.'

She ran an affectionate hand across my cheek as her other descended to the juncture of my thighs. She rubbed gently. Light as it was, I trembled at her touch. My quim seemed more sensitive than usual. 'Here?' said she.

'Yes,' said I, wondering dimly how she could know its location.

'Ah then, we will scratch if for you.

'Thank you, Lady Doris, but 'tis deep inside.' I felt a glow of gratitude.

'Fear not.' Sir Harry knelt by the settee; his hand, like a small and friendly beast, crawled under my skirt. 'We possess the ideal cure for such internal infirmities.'

Stretching languorously under their gentle explorations. I closed my eyes. They were indeed a most caring and gracious family.

After how long, I know not, I felt cool air on the naked flesh of my body. I opened my eyes on Bettina. She loomed over me, exuding a strong scent of musk and sandlewood as she busied herself undressing me. (It was, I thought, a strange and exotic odour for a serving girl.) As I watched through hooded eyes, she rolled down the tops of my bloomers, exposing my belly to the cooling atmosphere. Then with serious demeanour, she pulled them down all the way. I was naked, vulnerable, open!

'Ah, 'tis as I thought,' said Sir Harry. 'Delightful.'

'Indeed, she is,' said Lady Doris with a little laugh.

'Indeed,' I repeated mindlessly, flushing hot and cold in a sudden fit of lascivious desire.

'The drug has taken hold beautifully,' said Sir Harry.

'A most admirable substance,' said Lady Doris.

'Admirable substance,' I echoed. Their laughter pleased me. I joined them in it, little realizing that it was myself at whom they were laughing. The vague understanding that I'd been drugged seemed of no consequence; I was preoccupied with lust.

25

'Is there anything, dear Jenny, that you'd like?'

'Yes, milady.'

'And that is?'

'I would like to be fucked.' Though I was aware of hearing, rather than speaking them, they were my words, enunciated calmly, despite a near frenzy of desire that gripped me. 'Fucked,' I repeated the word, savouring the sound of it as if it were a sweetmeat.

'Bettina, Miss Everleigh is ready,' said Sir Harry. 'You may prepare her for me.'

'Thank you, sir,' said Bettina, kneeling by the side of the settee.

I heard my own passion-choked voice call out: 'Fuck me! Please, fuck me!' Then, as if launched by the words themselves: 'Fuck . . . fuck!' I felt I was about to drown in a turbulent sea of unrequited passion! 'Help me . . .'

Bettina grasped my ankles, elevated and spread my legs, bending my knees till they rested on my breasts. In a trice her pretty young head was between my thighs, her cool breath fanning my feverish, swollen pussy lips.

'Suck her,' said Sir Harry.

'Yessss,' said I, my voice, my entire body quivering in spasmodic expectation. 'Anything! Everything! Please.'

FOUR

There are many who find the concept of female pleasure inconcievable. They include the womanizer whose only interest is his own pleasure and the Christian who considers the very idea of pleasure to be sinful. Odd bedfellows indeed. [George Sand]

I emerged from blackness to find that someone was fucking me! My eyes opened on Sir Harry Fibbit's lust-contorted face. In a passionate frenzy, he was looming over me, pumping with long, powerful strokes. As consciousness returned I became aware that my body was responding, my hips thrusting upwards as he filled me, then rotating in tight tempestuous circles as his corpulent prick pulled back to cock itself for yet another plunge! How long, I wondered, had I been unconsciously engaged in this wildly choreographed dance of lust? My last recollection had been the delicious sensation of Bettina's tongue on my ferverish quim, then an instantaneous orgasmic explosion . . . then nothingness! Had I fainted?

The conjecture was lost in a wildfire of sensations, as now, once again, I was rapidly approaching the peak. Within seconds the tremors commenced, shooting through my body, communicating excruciating pleasure to every part of me: my breasts, the back of my neck, my belly . . . my very skin and the roots of my hair. Every part of me seemed even more sensitive, more responsive to pleasure than it had ever been! Then finally, with Sir Harry thrusting into me in ever-increasing tempo, I was overcome by an ecstatic detonation beyond any I had ever experienced! It became one with a series of exquisite aftershocks, each one slightly less intense than the one preceeding it. I was aware of my own voice crying out incoherently, of the wet slapping sounds of our fuckery, of Sir Harry's groans as my legs encircled his hips, securing his body to mine and locking his cock deep inside me. Then with our bodies still, I milked his tumescent organ with powerful cuntal contractions, its lustful proprietor moaning appreciation. Buried to the bollocks, its twitchings and throbbings created delicious, sympathetic tremors in my ravaged puss, till finally I was rewarded with my lover's loud, heartfelt groan of release. His body, atop my own, stiffened then trembled as if with a passionate ague. His cock, locked so deeply within me, seemed to grow even fatter. I thrilled as spasm after spasm racked Sir Harry's body, each of them accompanied by a gushing pulsation of creamy sperm!

'Bravo!' It was Lady Doris's voice.

From beneath Sir Harry's armpit, I glanced about. She was standing at the foot of the chaise. Grouped around her, all eyes glued to the fulcrum of our lust, were Bettina, Starns, and a short squat gentleman wearing a red fez. The fez was unusual in that it was the only piece of clothing in view. Both players and audience were naked!

As one, they looked up and applauded.

'Well done, Jenny,' said Lady Doris. 'You are truly a most accomplished fucker.'

'Here, here!' said Sir Harry, raising himself onto his elbows.

'Bravo,' said the gentleman in the fez. 'And, I might add, you are the most beautiful woman in all of England.'

'Thank you,' said I, blushing with embarrassment at the applause, the accolade.

'Doris, my dear,' said Sir Harry, his cock still twitching inside me, 'you must introduce our house guest.'

'Ah, yes,' said Lady Doris, 'forgive me.' With the fezzed

28

gentleman in tow, she stepped around to the side of the chaise. 'Miss Everleigh, I would like you to meet our house guest. Mr Aziz.'

'Charmed,' said he, with an oily grin.

I extended my hand. He brushed his lips across it in the manner of a true gentleman, then held it with bejewelled fingers, his dark eyes burning into mine.

'I'm happy to meet you,' said I, my glance straying downwards. His zubrik, hanging at rest below the fleshy proturberance of his belly, was circumcised — just as I thought it would be. 'I see you are a devout Moslem.'

'Ah, such perfection in a woman is a rare thing, indeed,' said Mr Aziz. 'I mean to say that you are not only accomplished and beautiful, but you also know our customs.' He smiled broadly, revealing a gold tooth. 'And do you approve, Miss Everleigh?'

'Wholeheartedly, Mr Aziz. I find such penile modification to be both a practical and aesthetic improvement over what nature has provided.'

'You leave me with no alternative, Miss Everleigh, than to react with pride.' His pego was stiffening.

'Manly pride, to be sure,' said I. 'To be sure,' said he, reached downward to grasp his half-hardened member. 'You seem to understand the men of Islam. Might I assume you've lived amongst us?'

'Not exactly, Mr Aziz. But I have had an Egyptian lover.' I felt tempted to tell him that the lover had been none other than the son of the khedive, Tewfik Pasha, soon to be ruler of Egypt (if Edward and the British foreign office had their way). But that would give things away. Mum's the word, thought I. I realized that the peculiar brain fever I'd experienced earlier had cleared. The cobwebs had dissipated and once again I was thinking with reasonable clarity.

'Ah, Jenny,' said Lady Doris, 'you become more interesting by the minute. Perhaps you will tell us about this exotic affair.'

29

'Perhaps,' said I enigmatically, recalling that she and Sir Harry had earlier made some reference to a drug. Such would certainly explain my recent, brief indisposition, the deep tingling itch I had felt in my vagina, the rabid, undirected desire that had come over me like a sudden fever. I had never once, in the past, fainted in the clutches of an orgasm. Surely, it was a drug that had multiplied the intensity of my usual lusty nature! Furthermore, thought I, Bettina's gamahuching, the vigorous fucking, and the two intense orgasms I had just experienced would ordinarily have satisfied me, at least for a time. But such was not the case. 'Twas as if all of it had been mere 'foreplay.' It was obvious that one effect of the drug had worn off but another remained. Once again I found myself trembling with lust.

In a single deft motion I rolled over, carrying my expended lover with me. Now, astride, it was I who was the rider and he the mount. Slowly I raised my hips. Sir Harry's cock emerged, rigid, glistening in the gaslight. It was my first view of the monstrous organ — fatter around than any I'd yet seen! I uncunted more and more of it, losing myself in the exquisitely piquant sensation of withdrawal.

As the corpulent mushroom of its head came into view, I glanced about to find our audience was once again observing the lewd junction. Still partially plugged, I squatted, as before our eyes, my champion went soft. Finally unable to sustain itself, the poor, shrunken, sodden affair plopped out of me. It lay sadly, minus even a hint of its former magnificence, on Sir Harry's hairy belly.

I looked up to see Lady Doris, her shapely bum poised over her husbands's face. In a quiet voice, she said, 'Harry, would you like to watch Starns fuck me while you recover your strength?'

'A captial idea, my darling.'

She bent forward, balancing herself against me, elevating her plump bottom as an offering to the butler.

'Fuck her, there's a good fellow,' said Sir Harry, his face just inches from his wife's hairy quim.

'Yes, sir,' said Starns, stepping forward smartly, as if he were obeying a military command.

Lady Doris glanced over her shoulder to observe the weirdly impassive butler grasp her hips. She turned, bringing her eyes just inches from mine. 'Ah, Jenny . . . he's entering me.' She held her breath, then released it in a long drawn-out sigh. 'Oh my dear, 'tis heavenly.'

Her lips sought out my breast. 'Heavenly,' I echoed.

'Ah,' said Sir Harry from beneath, 'He is half in you my dear . . . a most stimulating view.'

I glanced to my left. Bettina was on her knees, her pretty little mouth sucking gently on Mr Aziz's stiffened pego. She glanced at me out of the corner of her eye, then removing Mr Aziz's weapon from her mouth to hold it in a proprietory grip, she said, 'I'm readying him for you, Miss Jenny.'

'Thank you, Bettina,' said I, touched.

'You're most welcome, mum.'

Lady Doris nibbled on the erect nub of my nipple, sending little shocks of delight coursing through my body. A whimper escaped her lips as slowly the butler's prick filled her seething pussy. With that accomplished, he drew back, withdrawing inch after inch of rigid cockshaft. Finally, when only the head remained inserted, he paused, his body cocked as if it were a powerful longbow poised to launch an enchanted arrow.

Lady Doris, her eyes closed, her breath stilled in ecstatic expectation, desengaged herself from my breast. From between her thighs, Sir Harry's voice boomed., 'Thrust home, Starns!'

As if he had been awaiting his master's order, the lustful butler did just that. With a single, powerful movement of his hips, he drove his prick in to the hilt! Lady Doris threw her head back, her breath exploding in a sharp squeal as his muscular belly slapped against the pneumatic flesh of her buttocks.

I was almost overcome by a sudden, sympathetic fit of

31

lust as Sir Harry's hand exploring blindly, found my fervid cunt. Lady Doris pressed her open lips to mine, fucking my mouth with her tongue in tempo with Starn's powerful thrustings. Her fingers pinched my nipples.

'Miss Everleigh . . .' 'Twas the voice of Mr Aziz. I turned to see him stretched out on the floor now, Bettina still servicing his rampant zubrik.

'Would you care to join us, dear lady?' said he.

'I'd be delighted,' said I, breathlessly, as Sir Harry rolled my clitty between a gentle thumb and forefinger.

Lady Doris, her curvaceous bottom rotating about the fulcrum of the butler's cock, spoke in a voice hoarse with lust. 'Ah, dear Jenny, you will just adore being fucked by Mr Aziz.'

I disconnected myself from husband and wife to squat on the floor beside Bettina. With her saucy eyes on mine she licked the full length of Mr Aziz's swollen organ. 'Twas indeed a most fetching sight; she manoeuvred her lovely pink tongue with talent and sensitivity. As I watched, salivating, she circumnavigated the underside of the bulbous cockhead. Mr Aziz trembled, groaned in appreciation. Bettina grasped the delicious thing in her hand and, like a child offering her playmate a succulent sweetmeat, held it to my eager lips.

I flicked my tongue under the head. It seemed to shudder in Bettina's grip as its proprietor, Mr Aziz, placed his hands atop my head, entangling his fingers in my hair. My eyes were closed, my lips wet with lubricating saliva. Bettina let go as I approached his weapon from the side, frigging back and forth with my open mouth.

I felt Bettina's hand on my breast. Then she was facing me, her lips parted, sharing Mr Aziz's rampant cock with me as he thrust his hips back and forth. His weapon was caught alternately, in the tender trap of our soft, open lips. Except for the interceding male organ, it was as if we were kissing one another.

The suggestion seemed to make itself known to us

simultaneously. In tandem, we deserted the male object of our affection. Our lips met but a half inch above Mr Aziz's cock. Her tongue was between my lips, caressing mine. Enthralling! Her hand cupped my breast, its thumb moving back and forth, gently, over the distended nipple. It was all so soft . . . lovely . . . different than a man would be . . . her lips more supple, her tongue more gracefully erotic. There was no hardness, no feeling of strength. I shivered with quiet rapture. I reached out tentative fingers to fondle her breasts . . . smooth, tight-skinned, luscious rotundities! She flushed with ardour, sighed into my open mouth.

All the while our free hands were gently pumping the Arab's erect penis. I held him with two fingers encircling just beneath the purple helmet. Bettina had the rest of him ensconced within the confines of her fist. He groaned, tried to sit up. I abandoned Bettina's lips to take half the length into my mouth. In a trice, Bettina was licking his bollocks.

I was burning with lust. My arse waved in mid air, undulating as if in reaction to a phantom pego buried deep in my seething puss. I sucked deeply, taking him to the portals of my throat – then beyond. His hips pumped desperately, fucking my face.

Now, Bettina was with me again. She fondled my breasts, pinched my turgid nipples. I felt her soft tongue in my ear, her hot sweet breath on my cheeks, made plump with cock. 'Twas a cock I gave up once again in order to kiss her. Her soft lips thrilled me! Her searching tongue sent rivers of rapture through my body.

I straddled Mr Aziz as the lusful maid gripped his weapon, aligning it with its lascivious target. With my quim awash in welcoming juices, I descended slowly, thrilled by the sight of the long, hard muscular pole. In . . . in! I squatted, suspended above him as he fucked upward, deeper and deeper with each stroke; pulling the soft cunt-flesh inward. I felt Bettina's fingers at the juncture, caressing, stroking the erect nodule of my clitoris.

Her hand was trapped between our quivering bodies as I

took the full length of Mr Aziz's proud cock. His wiry pubic hair entangled with my silken pubic tresses as I pressed my body downward, rotating my arse in tight circles.

'Sit on his face Bettina,' said I breathlessly, into her open mouth. 'Sit . . . squat on his face so that he may suck you.

'May I?'

'Please . . . yes.' said Mr Aziz, moaning, as I treated him to a series of cunning contractions.

Bettina flicked my clit one last time before removing her hand from between our interlocked groins. In a trice she was straddling Mr Aziz's head. His hands curled about her waist, supporting her as she lowered her feverish body.

She squashed her luscious cunt over his mouth, a sight that sent tremors of passion through my body. I began pumping up and down, short deep strokes that became longer and longer. Soon, the upward thrusts were almost uncunting his fat zubrik and the downward plunges slapped our groins together. Bettina and I fondled each other's breasts as once again she leaned forward, offering me her tongue to suck.

We remained that way: I bouncing up and down on Mr Aziz's cock; she, squirming about on his face. The three of us caressing, kissing, squeezing, licking, sucking, fucking!

Hearing a cry of passion from my left, I recalled that we were not the only trio in the morning room. Out of the corner of my eye I perceived a tableau even more lascivious than our own!

Still on the chaise, with her well-rounded arse elevated for the carnal convenience of the butler, Lady Doris lay atop her husband. His prick had once again stiffened into formidable proportions. She sucked it passionately whilst, with his head situated conveniently in the erogenous junction between her plump thighs, he alternately licked her clitoris and tongued the length of her lover's pistoning cock! It was indeed, an inspired vision of marital bliss beyond any I had ever witnessed!

The tension in my own body was building. Breaking the kiss, I looked into Bettina's eyes. They opened wide to stare into mine, unblinking. 'Tell me,' said I.

'Ah, 'tis lewd,' said the little maid, her hips jerking back and forth, her clit between the Arab's lips. 'Lovely . . . And you, Miss Jenny?'

'Yesss,' said I. 'Lovely . . .' His body beneath mine was thrusting upward as my arse screwed, first one way then the other, taking his cock deep inside my suctioning pussy. There were little whimpering sounds, mine and Bettina's. Our mutual lover groaned mightily.

'Oh suck me, sir,' said Bettina.

'Cush!' he cried, burying his face deeper in her oozing shrine.

'Fuck!' I cried.

'Zigazig!' groaned the Arab, his voice muffled in cuntflesh, his tongue alternately beating her clit and lapping within the soft, saturated folds of her labia.

I flicked my fingers over her nipples, then pinched hard. She did likewise. I felt about to explode.

'Now?' she asked. 'Now, Miss Jenny?'

'Soon.' I could feel her trembling even as I did likewise. 'And you, Bettina?'

'Soon . . . ahhh!'

I felt at one with her. Mr Aziz, the mutual instrument of our passion, squirmed mightily. His body stiffened as I pressed downward, taking him all; milking him with my powerful cuntal muscles. I felt his cock twitching.

'He's about to cum,' I murmured into her mouth.

'Oh, miss, he's fucking me with his tongue . . . 'tis all the way inside me!'

'Cummm,' I whispered.

'Yes, I'm there. I'm cumming, Miss Jenny!'

I held her tightly, feeling her body quiver as Mr Aziz's

cock, deep inside me, convulsed, squirting what felt to be a fountain of jism!

'He's shooting,' I cried. 'I can feel him squirting . . . ahhh Bettina!' The cuntal tremors were spreading throughout my body, building to a climax.

Her pretty pink tongue caressed my lower lip. I sucked it into my mouth as Mr Aziz spurted, again and again.

'I'm cumming, Bettina!'

'Oh do, Miss Jenny!'

The orgasm burst within me like a monstrous display of fireworks! I was fragmented, each minute part of me ablaze in ecstasy! It seemed an eternity before I finally coalesced.

'Oh, Miss Jenny,' she sobbed. We clutched at each other, collapsed in each other's arms as all movement ceased.

FIVE

Society has decreed that women be the reward for chivalrous behaviour but never its perpetrator. Of this, the stuff of romance is made. [Henry James]

That night, as I was about to drift off into a well-deserved sleep, there was a light, surreptitious tapping on my door. Throwing on a dressing gown (I always sleep nude), I opened the door to find the young Noel Fibbit holding a bottle of champagne and two glasses.

He spoke in tones just above a whisper. 'Good evening, Miss Everleigh.'

'Good evening, Noel,' said I, immediately aware of his obvious intent.

'May I come in?'

'I don't think so; it's late. I'm quite tired.'

He smiled self-consciously. 'Yes. I heard you had a busy day.'

'Indeed, 'twas most busy.'

'Bettina told me. She thinks highly of you.'

'And I of her.'

'Please?' A desperate entreaty furrowed his youthful brow. 'I brought champagne.'

'I see.' I smiled pleasantly. 'And you're here to make love to me.'

'Yes.' He studied his shoes.

'I'm flattered, dear Noel, but your father insisted that you are not to attempt such a thing until you have honoured your commitment to deflower your young lady, Miss Deborah MacDill. First things first, he said. A proper young man must dedicate himself to his stated goals; he must develop self-discipline, play the game, and all that sort of thing. Your father is devoted to your character development. I couldn't allow myself to be an instrument of your disobedience.'

'But my father does not have to know.'

'I am a guest in his house, Noel.' I placed my hand on his arm. 'Such deception on my part would be unseemly. And besides, surely it won't be that long before you have accomplished your purpose with Miss MacDill.'

'Perhaps not,' said he, his voice cracking.

Speaking brightly, I said. 'And afterwards I myself will be your reward for a job well done. You will find me all the sweeter for the waiting.'

He smiled weakly. 'Well then, perhaps we should drink on it. A nightcap?'

'And that's all?' said I.

'Yes.'

'On your honour as a gentleman?'

'Yes . . . on my honour as a gentleman.'

I stepped aside, allowing him to enter. There could be no harm in a nightcap. I sat primly on the chair, he on the bed. He said nothing, concentrating on opening the bottle. He seemed startled by the loud pop, then awkward as he poured – all thumbs. Somehow, he managed to spill not a drop as he handed me a glass.

Finally, he looked up. His voice wavered nervously as if he were delivering a rehearsed speech. 'You are. I think, the most beautiful woman I have ever set eyes on.'

His infatuation was obvious. In order to change the subject, I raised my glass, saying gaily. 'Do you know the origin of the champagne glass?'

'I'm afraid not.'

'The original was made from a mould of Marie Antoinette's left breast.'

38

He stared glumly into his champagne. 'I would give my all to posses a glass moulded from *one of yours*.'

'Your all, Master Noel?' said I. 'For something you've never seen?'

'But I have, indeed . . .'

'No.'

'Most assuredly, dear Miss Jenny; a beautiful breast, a breast beyond description, matched by only one other – its twin.'

'But how?'

'The orgy in the morning room; I observed the proceedings from beginning to end.'

'But, you weren't there.'

'Ah, but I was near,' said Noel Fibbit, downing his bubbly in one nervous gulp. 'I was hidden – a secret place.'

I stared at him over the rim of my glass. 'You naughty boy!'

He blushed. 'I love to watch. I have been doing it since I was a child.'

'Do your parents know of this?'

'No. You're the first person to whom I've ever mentioned it.'

'But where . . .?'

'Inside – between – the walls, dear Jenny. There are passageways, secret spaces, all connected.' His voice took on a feverish note of pride as if he were describing a brilliant personal accomplishment. 'I can move about in secret and peek into more than half the rooms in this house – nineteen of them, in fact.'

Surely, thought I, he has made it all up; an infatuated young man inventing a fantastic story to impress me. But then again? I gestured about me. 'Here too?'

'Of course.'

'Show me.'

He stood abruptly, paced to the far side of my bedroom. 'It's been my secret alone since I discovered it when I was just a boy: the secret passageways and chambers, the peepholes . . . all of it. I will show you this, but no more. Agreed?'

'Agreed,' said I, crossing my fingers.

An ornate sconce grew from the wall on either side of the mantel. He pointed enigmatically to the one on the right. 'Here,' he said.

Examining it carefully, I observed a small opening. It was barely a quarter inch in diameter, concealed cunningly in the ornately carved filigree. 'Good Lord, 'tis true,' said I. I felt a sudden excitement. A means actually existed to observe throughout the house without being observed in turn! Surely this would be an invaluable tool in my secret investigation of Sir Harry!

He placed his hand on my arm. 'You must tell no one Miss Jenny – please.'

''Twill be our secret, Noel,' said I, feeling a growing excitement.

'Swear it.'

'I do.'

'Yes, but you must actually swear *on* something.'

'On my breasts,' said I, knowing how he valued them. 'I swear on my breasts that I will reveal your secret to no one.'

'May I feel them?'

'Of course,' said I, turning to him. I calmed myself, realizing that I must play the game carefully in order to extract all the information I could about the diabolical secret architecture of Fanshawe House. My tactic: advance and retreat, submit and deny.

He extended both hands to run tentative fingers across the tops of my twin rotundities. Then with his eyes closed, he cupped them, squeezing gently. Though I could feel the heat of his palms through the silk of my dressing gown, my growing excitement had little to do with physical pleasure. 'Twas his passion, not mine that must be raised to fever pitch. I allowed him to play amongst the hillocks for a few more moments, then grasping his wrists, I said. 'Do my breasts still meet with your approval?'

'A thousand times over.' Sighing deeply, he took both my hands in his. 'I love you, dearest Miss Jenny.'

'How nice of you,' said I, kissing him lightly on his cheek. 'But we must still honour your father's wishes.'

He stepped back dejectedly. 'Yes . . . of course.'

'But I do want to thank you for sharing your secret with me.' I placed my hand on the back of his neck. As he turned I pressed my lips to his. 'I feel I should reward you.' I muttered, spreading my lips to welcome his insistent tongue. 'A foretaste of the pleasures to come once you have fulfilled your previous commitment . . .'

His hands descended the length of my back to cup my buttocks as they had cupped my breasts just moments before. He pressed me tightly against him. I could feel his stiffening manhood through layers of clothing.

I spoke calmly. 'How does one get inside?'

'Quite simply, I believe,' he said, reaching about to insert his hand into the opening of my gown.

'No, dear Noel,' said I. 'I mean inside the walls.' I placed my hand on his, locking it against the smooth flesh of my thigh.

'There are seven secret entrances.'

'Where?'

'As I told you, I will reveal no more.'

I sighed aloud for his benefit. My game, I realized, was all but won. 'Of course,' I said, dispiritedly. 'How could I expect you to trust me?' His fingers flexed on my thighs as I pressed my body against his.

''Tis not a matter of *me* trusting *you*,' said he, a note of petulance creeping into his voice. 'Quite the other way around, actually.'

I forced my groin against a now massive bulge. 'Despite everything, Noel dearest, I find it difficult to resist you.' I pulled away from him abruptly. 'But I must.'

'Please, Jenny. You're driving me mad!' With his hands grasping my buttocks, he pulled me back.

'Poor boy,' said I sweetly. I could feel his hardened cock,

the instrument of my will, twitching mightily as if attempting to force its way through the heavy material of his trousers.

'I've got to have you . . . now.!'

'If you do,' said I quietly, rotating my hips, 'will you promise, as I did, that you will say nothing to anyone?'

'Never, my sweet.'

'Then, shall we also say that it is a matter of mutual trust?' I stepped back, taking both his hands in mine, engaging his eyes. 'A matter of opening for opening? Yours for mine?'

'Yes,' he croaked.

Once again I presented my lips. 'And so?' said I, muttering into his open mouth.

He swallowed deeply. 'There is one in this very room.'

Noel Fibbit turned about. Then, kneeling by the fireplace, he said, 'Third brick from the bottom. One presses it in, thusly . . .' He reached into the fireplace to push the indicated brick inward. Then, grasping a poker, he brought it to bear against one side of the rear firewall. The fire, which had been banked, flared briefly from a sudden draft. With a creak, a section of the wall opened on rusty hinges: a secret door large enough to crawl through. 'Unfortunately,' said he, 'this particular entrance is somewhat crude. I rarely use it as it leaves one filthy with soot.'

Repressing my excitement. I knelt beside him to peer into the mysterious darkness. 'And from here?'

'From here one can go all about, inside the walls. 'Tis all interconnected: passageways, secret staircases, chambers, peepholes, other entrances. I'm not even sure I've explored all of it myself.'

'It's diabolical.'

'Quite.' Hooking the end of the poker into a protuberance in the firewall, he pulled it closed. It latched with a loud click and the loose brick snapped back into position. There was a small cloud of dust but naught else to indicate an opening.

As Noel got to his feet. I stepped back and with a deft motion unhooked my gown. It slipped from my shoulders, revealing the plump flesh of my breasts. 'A bargain is a bargain,' said I, my voice hoarse with promise.

'Lovely . . .'

'Now we will share the second intimate secret.'

'Yes, let's do,' he whispered, reaching for me.

'No . . . just watch.' I moved back another step, allowing the gown to slither down the length of my body.

Noel stood, spellbound, his hands at his side. His eyes descended, surveying every inch of naked flesh as it was revealed. Naked, the gown a silken pool at my feet, I placed my hand between my thighs. Under the breathless intensity of his gaze, I inserted my finger deep into my vagina. 'And this, dear Noel, is *my* secret entrance.' Slowly, I withdrew the finger, then placed it, dampened with cuntal honey, to his lips. As he sucked on it I stepped into his arms. A bargain was, indeed, a bargain.

He was atop me in a moment, plunging desperately even before I had him inserted. It was over quickly. In what seemed to be a matter of seconds, Noel exploded inside me. 'Twas a copious injection, but unfortunately a premature one. Poor Noel . . .

Built in 1782 by Sir Harry Fibbit's maternal grandfather, Lord Fanshawe, the house on Marston Moor was a Georgian mansion of some thirty-two rooms. Sometime in the recent past Sir Harry had closed off the west wing, leaving just twenty-three, including the servant's quarters, which housed a butler, a head housekeeper, a cook, a pantry boy, a kitchen maid, a scullery maid, three housemaids, a lady's maid, a gentleman's valet, a gardener, a liveryman, and a coachman.

Its proprietor, my employer, Sir Harry Fibbit, was quite well preserved and looked to be fifteen years younger than his actual age of sixty at least. Sir Harry was a jovial and robust gentleman, an epicurean intellectual, a true satyr.

Despite the fact that he and his wife had drugged me the previous day, I found it hard to believe him the villain painted by the Prince of Wales. But then, my experience with real villains was limited. Till now, I had known but a single one.

On my first morning, after breakfasting with the family, Sir Harry announced that it was time to acquaint me with my duties as editor of his memoirs. He showed me into his study and then, with his trousers around his knees and my skirt thrown up over my arse, proceeded to fuck me on the large walnut desk.

Afterwards, with the utmost decorum, he introduced me to the diaries, letters, and journals that I was to transcribe sequentially and arrange in manuscript form. It seemed to my inexperienced eye to be a job that would require months to complete. My salary, he stated, was to be the sum of one-pound-six per week. Arrangements would be made to have some of my things shipped up from my London flat. With that he left me to my first day's work.

I spent the morning, and after a spot of lunch brought to me on a tray, the afternoon, acquainting myself with my employer's diaries, letters, and journals. Except for an occasional political or philosophic digression, they seemed to concern themselves mainly with Sir Harry's amatory adventures.

It appeared that my employer was a man of many talents: a raconteur, an inventor, an author, a philospher, a true lover of women. However, being a gentleman, and the women in question, for the most part, being ladies, Sir Harry did not reveal actual identities. Nevertheless, he took great pride in having pleasured, amongst many others, a (nameless) Empress of France; the young wives of two (nameless) elderly Tory cabinet ministers and the daughter of one of them by another marriage; three nameless sisters, ladies-in-waiting to a (nameless) Czarina; a (nameless) member of the British royal family; the (nameless) niece of a current Pope of Rome, and the redheaded

44

wife of a (nameless) American vice-president. This is but a minuscule sampling of almost a hundred conquests, dealt with in Sir Harry Fibbit's papers. (I leave it to my esteemed readers to unravel these deliciously scandalous puzzles. Like Sir Harry, I have included sufficient clues.)

It was clear from his writings that this intellectual satyr valued the company of ladies at least as much as any lady has ever valued the company of gentlemen. He was happiest in their presence; he not only liked women, but equally important, his attitude towards them was modified with neither artifice nor lack of understanding. His greatest gratification came from giving them pleasure. (Having been personally involved, I can vouch for the fact that in this most important of callings he was masterful.) A rare man, he even understood female logic.

Sir Harry, in his memoirs, seemed equally proud of his wife's achievements. Though he did not deal with them as extensively as with his own conquests, he did delineate them in his diaries. This was especially true when his wife's assignations afforded him an observation post. With her collusion, he had hidden in closets and trunks, behind drapes and under beds. Disguised as a hackman, he had once observed his wife and a member of the Swedish royal house through the trap of a hansom cab. In a Bavarian castle he had observed from inside an ornamental suit of armour. In a grand hotel in the American city of Philadelphia he had observed his wife's pleasuring from the floor below through the use of a cunning brass periscope, custom-made for him by E. Cook and Sons, Ltd.

My wife, he wrote proudly, *has been ploughed by the great and the near great of five continents*. Indeed, if one used sheer numbers as a criterion, she had outdone him.

Unlike his own conquests, Sir Harry Fibbit had no scruples about naming names when it came to his wife's male lovers. *Women may be sacrosanct*, wrote he, *but it is not the prerogative of a gentleman to protect the names of other gentlemen in such situations.*

Amongst her conquests, were the Crown Prince of Japan, the King of Bavaria, the mayor of Philadelphia, the governor general of Australia, King Tshombo of the Matabeli Tribe, the Yankee general William Tecumseh Sherman, the great Spanish matador Jorge Mateo, the American poet Edgar Allan Poe, the Italian composer Giuseppe Verdi, the French doctor Louis Pasteur, two Hapsburgs, a Windsor, four Romanoffs, (three of them simultaneously!), and a rather elderly Rothschild.

And, wrote Sir Harry Fibbit, *she has experienced lascivious congress with almost as many women as have I, her loving husband.*

And then, these words:

We, man and wife, are living monuments to nineteenth-century arts, letters and history. Between us we have sown our English seed, our essence, our sexuality amongst the nobility, the leaders, the intellectuals, the artists, the rare and fair beauties (and their spouses) of all the continents. We have demonstrated the superiority of British amatory powers and lustful invention over all others. In the best of all possible worlds we would be honoured for our service to the empire and perhaps a momument: a towering phallus, flanked at the base with two rotund British lions, would be erected to celebrate our noble and proud achievement. Surely we have accomplished as much as those other explorers – Burton, Speke, Stanley. God save the Queen!'

Was he mad? I paused in my conjecture. Even more important, was Sir Harry Fibbit a traitor to his country? I reminded myself that my true job was to deal with that possibility. It was time to get on with it.

On my second night in residence at Fanshawe House, after making sure that my bedroom door was locked, I manipulated the secret brick beneath the mantel. The small hidden door at the rear of the fireplace sprung open and I crawled through to stand erect for the first time in the dark and mysterious world between its walls. The passageway in which I found myself was not very much wider than my own body. I was aware of a musty odour: an ancient, stagnant atmosphere barely adequate to sustain the flame of my single candle. The flickering light revealed no more than a few feet of the narrow passageway, which extended into a morbid and portentous blackness.

At my shoulder, a heavy iron lever grew out of the stone. Gingerly, I reached up to pull it and was rewarded with a groan of metal on stone. My assumption as to its function was correct. The square patch of light that was my bedroom disappeared. My last contact with the real world had winked out.

I stood for a moment, attemtping to screw up the courage necessary to continue my exploration. Surely, I thought, my fear was irrational. I breathed deeply. There was a scurrying sound, a stirring in the darkness . . . mice? My skin crawled with horror. Rats? In a state of panic I pushed upward on the iron lever. In a trice I was through the resultant opening, to stand, breathless, in the more congenial air of my bedroom.

Using a poker, as my young paramour had demonstrated, I hurriedly pulled closed the secret hatch. Then, seated stiffly on the dge of the bed, I stared fixedly at the fireplace.

Spying, as it turned out, required action for which I had little stomach. Had I known that my activities would include such purely masculine pursuits as messing about in a horrifying maze of dark passageways that were crawling with rodents, I would have advised the Prince of Wales that perhaps someone else would be better suited. My courage, I realized, was simply not adequate to the task. 'Twas indeed a pity; for to observe, I conjectured, without being observed in turn, should certainly be the dream of any spy worth his salt. But nevertheless, there seemed

47

nothing for it but for me to abandon the tool placed so providentially in my hands. I was, when all was said and done, only a woman.

'Only a woman,' I repeated aloud, minutes later, as I lay on my bed, staring at the ceiling. A man, acting as I had, would have been considered a coward. But as a woman, I had no fear of such a stigma; the term *cowardice* is never applied to us. Women (particularly gentlewomen) are not expected to act boldy in the face of terror. (In fact, we are actually encouraged to do the opposite.) It is generally accepted that women are hysterical, incapable of such male attributes as leadership, logical thought, or physical courage. We are considered the weaker sex. Bravery, valour, gallantry are functions of manliness. It is a woman's duty to encourage such masculine behaviour (often on her own behalf), not to practise it.

Surely, thought I, all of this was rational justification for my recent action. Since society demanded not of me that I be fearless in such circumstances, then why should I be?

But what of Joan of Arc? Florence Nightingale? Queen Elizabeth? Or for that matter, what of myself: Jenny Everleigh, Chevalier of the Legion of Honour? Had not the Empress Eugénie herself cited me for having risked my life in the commission of 'an act of courage equal to that of any man?'* Yet alas, here I sat, just a year later, afraid of the dark and terrified of mice!

It was all very obvious: either I admitted inferiority and reconciled myself to being only a woman, or I admitted cowardice. If it were the latter, then there was no alternative but to return the white feather by going back into the walls of Fanshawe House!

I felt a growing anger at first at the concept of female inferiority and then at myself. Shame! It was a simple thing indeed to hide behind the scented facade of female stereotype. I had made a commitment to the son of my

See Book One. The Intimate Memoir of Dame Jenny Everleigh.

sovereign. Male *or* female, turning from it was nothing less than an act of cowardice!

Without lending another thought to the matter, I rose up from my bed.

SIX

We are not amused. [Queen Victoria]

Again, candle in hand, I found myself in the narrow passageway beween the walls of Fanshawe House. Once again I pulled the lever, leaving behind the secure familiarity of my bedroom. Disregarding the prickling in the back of my neck, I made my way forward.

The wall to my right was constructed of wood, to my left of dank grey stone. After a while the narrow passageway ended in a cul-de-sac. As I got closer however, it became evident that the facing wall, made of brick, actually marked a junction. Another passageway bisected my own, continuing at right angles, in both directions.

I turned left – an arbitary decision – to find myself in a passageway somewhat wider than the one I had just left. Where, I wondered, with growing trepidation, were the peepholes of which Noel Fibbit had spoken? Where were the other secret entrances? With measured steps I arrived at a second junction, this time a single passageway opened to the right. I disregarded it and continued straight on.

When I was a child, darkness had a tendency to distort time, to stretch minutes into hours while I lay in bed wondering fearfully what horror lurked beneath it. Now, as a grown woman I felt a similar disorientation. How long had I been between the walls of Fanshawe House? Thirty minutes? An hour? My candle indicated otherwise; it had burned down hardly at all.

Again, the scurrying and squeaking of invisible rodents raised my hackles. Fear begets fear ... a deep chill of anxiety froze me in my tracks. Surely some unspeakable malignancy lay just beyond the flickering amber glow of my pitiful candle! With that thought, every muscle in my body grew tense, willing me to turn about and be done with it. No! I steeled myself. I would not give in to irrational terror! Onward! In for a penny, in for a pound.

My next step was into thin air! The solid flooring beneath me was no more. I was falling! A woman screamed! Down I plummeted, arms and legs flailing, down into black and empty space! The scream was mine! It was cut short by a sudden and stunning blow to my backside as I struck bottom!

I was dead! But no, there was a sharp pain in my left ankle – a sign of life. I was stunned, breathless. It seemed a full minute before I opened eyes that served me not at all. I was lying, doubled up, on a hard and alien floor in total darkness. With an effort of will, I fought back a second scream. My candle was gone.

I lay gathering my wits. I must take stock. My left leg was double up beneath me. Gingerly, I grasped the calf to straighten it. A shock of pain raced from ankle to knee. Breathing deeply, I fought back a fit of sobbing. Was it broken? Cautiously, I wriggled my toes. Broken bones or no, I could not lie there till I starved to death ... or worse, till I was attacked and murdered – eaten alive – by rats!

I pulled myself along the filthy floor until, after a few feet, my head made contact with the wall. It was wood. I edged along it till a vertical beam came to hand. I grasped, pulled myself erect, wincing with pain from inadvertent pressure on my bad ankle. For a full minute, eyes clamped shut, I stood, breathing deeply, recovering from the effort. Supporting my weight on one leg, I turned to rest my back against the wall. 'What now, Jenny?' I spoke the words aloud, hearing them as if they'd been enunciated by someone else. This time I opened my eyes on a spot of light. No larger than a shilling piece, it seemed afloat in the blackness.

If my orientation was intact – a doubtful prospect – and if I could assume that the passageway, in which I now stood, was not very much wider than the one from which I had fallen, and if I were not actually looking down the length of a long connecting corridor, then the light must be coming from the opposite wall. An affirmative answer to each of the ifs would, I conjectured, indicate a peephole, no further than four or five feet from where I stood.

Praying that I would not fall through yet another opening in the floor, I made my way across the intervening distance in a single hop, though I ended up crumpled at the base of the opposite wall. There above me, was the spot of light. 'Twas indeed a peephole!

I stood, again like a stork, balanced on one leg. The peephole was at eye level, a small hole drilled through the wood. I pressed an eager eye to it.

'Twas a bedchamber, half again as large as my own, lit at the moment with two bedside candles and a fire in the grate. My point of view was toward the foot of the bed. The room was furnished tastefully and sported a polished, wooden wainscot that graced the lower third of the floral papered walls. A big, open steamer trunk occupied one corner. A cheval mirror near the far wall provided a second view of the bed. On it, half reclining against two large pillows, was Mr Aziz. He was naked, his eyes closed, his right hand gently stroking a handsome, semi-erect pego.

As I watched, a plan began formulating itself in my mind. I would wait until he was asleep, then crawl through his bedchamber and out the door. With luck I could get to my own room without being seen by anyone. (If I were seen, what possible excuse could I render that would explain my dishevelled appearance, my incapacitated ankle?)

Of course the plan depended on the existence of a secret entrance to Mr Aziz's bedchamber. I moved immediately to find it. Using the wall for support, I worked my way first to the left and with each halting step ran my hands down the length of the wall. After six or seven feet, I returned to where I had started and emplored to the right. In a trice, I found it! 'Twas an iron lever, near the floor similar to the one lending access to my own room. There was nothing for it now but to wait for Mr Aziz to fall asleep.

I returned to the peephole. He was still at it. As I watched he turned his head toward the door. The knock had been too faint for me to hear but it was obvious that someone was there.

'Come in,' he said, in a voice loud enough to pierce my wooden barricade.

'Twas Bettina. She was dressed in her usual maid's regalia. Before my eyes, Mr Aziz's prick, as if in instantaneous anticipation, rose to full extension. 'Ah, my nightly treatment, at last,' he said brightly, grasping his pego. 'I thought you weren't coming. How would I have fallen to sleep?'

'I'm sorry to be late,' said Bettina demurely. 'Lady Doris required my services and I –'

'All's well that ends well, as you English say.'

'Indeed, Mr Aziz.' She removed her shoes to climb onto the bed. 'We wouldn't want you to lie awake all night, turning and tossing.'

'You are a most charming and thoughtful young woman.'

'Thank you, sir.'

Without another word, Bettina positioned herself between his legs. Her novel slit skirt swung open to reveal a plump and shapely bottom. 'Twas as usual, a delightful sight, one that I certainly would have appreciated even more under more propitious circumstances. In the mirror I observed as she grasped the base of his member and swallowed it whole. Even from my blind I could see her cheeks bulging. Lovely, indeed. Then slowly, she brought her head up, releasing him bit by bit from the confines of her suctioning mouth until once again, the now glistening tool was free.

'Ah, I am in paradise,' said Mr Aziz, sighing deeply. 'You are a marvel, Bettina.'

'Thank you kindly, sir.' She snaked her tongue about the head, then lapped at the underside as if she were a child at the seashore enjoying a bit of Brighton rock.

My view of the bed enabled me to observe Mr Aziz's toes curling. The toenails were long, like the talons of a large bird. She began frigging him slowly as a sudden fatigue washed over me. I removed my eye from the peephole and lowered myself to the floor.

I stared into the darkness. From my experience with her, I agreed with Mr Aziz that Bettina was indeed a *marvel*. She was that and more. I wished her well. The sooner she accomplished her purpose the better for mine.

Though the sound was muffled through the wooden partition, I could hear Mr Aziz's groans. Seated, my back against the wall, I waited. Time passed . . . perhaps five minutes, perhaps ten. Surely the mad Turk must be approaching his release. Impatiently, I hoisted myself once again to the peephole.

In the mirror, Bettina, with consummate skill, was mouth-fucking Mr Aziz, causing his tumescent tool to piston in and out of her oval lips with ever-increasing tempo. Her left hand was buried in the crevice between his arse cheeks. Though I couldn't see it, I assumed a finger or two to be buried deep in the forbidden tunnel; massaging that secret, hidden male organ known only to a relatively few knowledgeable women. Her other arm was outstretched, its fingers busily engaged in tweaking and pinching one of Mr Aziz's nipples – yet another lascivious activity unknown to less sophisticated women.

Under ordinary circumstances a view such as this would have had me randy. But these were far from ordinary circumstances. Unfortunately, dear reader, my preoccupation left little room for the usual joys of lasivious voyeurism.

Nevertheless I still retained the facility to admire artistic talent, an attribute that even now was being put to use before my very eyes by a highly skilful and dedicated young woman.

Mr Aziz was very close. He was flexing his toes, groaning deep in his throat. Bettina grasped the base of his shaft and with the bulbous cock head clasped between her lips, was pumping him rapidly. Then, as his arse began to undulate, she grasped tight and sucked. A dollop of thick cream oozed from between her lips.

A minute later, job done, she was sitting on the edge of the bed putting on her shoes. Mr Aziz raised himself onto one elbow. 'Thank you, Bettina, my dear. I shall sleep well now.'

''Twas my pleasure, Mr Aziz.'

'Till tomorrow night, then . . . if not sooner.'

'Of course, kind sir.'

Patting her hair into place, she was out the door. Mr Aziz, obviously exhausted, turned onto his side. I lowered myself to the floor, once again, to wait him out.

Sometime later, I pulled the lever to open a sliding panel in the wainscoting. Then, to the unharmonious accompaniment of Mr Aziz's snores, I made my way through the small opening. Minutes passed while I searched for the outside latching device that would close it behind me. It was in the form of a small recessed lever, hidden beneath the wainscot rail.

I had crawled halfway to the door before it occurred to me that my plan was flawed. With a shock, I remembered that I had locked my own bedroom door from the inside!

What now? I crouched on the floor, my mind a muddle. There was only one answer to my problem. I forced myself to face it . . . back I must go into the dark and menacing secret passageways. 'Twas the only way I could return to my own room without giving everything away!

Mr Aziz's bedside candle was still alight. I took it with me back into the darkness.

The opening through which I had fallen was access for a ladder. I stood, supporting myself against it. Somehow, despite my crippled leg; I must climb ten or eleven feet with a candle in one hand. How?

Reaching up as far as I could, I put the candlestick on one of the rungs. I would place it higher as I progressed. Then, steeling myself for the ordeal, I positioned my good foot on the bottom rung.

The climb proved to be a slow and excruciating process. Despite the use of my arms, it entailed placing weight, at every step, on my bad ankle. 'Twas will alone that kept me from fainting. I took deep breaths, concentrating fully on the next step up . . . each rung a major victory.

Finally, at the top, I lay on the floor recovering my strength. Then as I made my way, using the wall for support, I found that my earlier fear had evaporated. The darkness seemed now to be nothing more than an inconvenience, the squeals and scurryings of little creatures, unmenacing. It required less than five minutes to make my way back to my room. Miraculously, my sense of time had been restored and I realized that with both legs intact, the outgoing voyage must have taken less than half that time. Ah, what strange tricks a terror-stricken mind can play! A strange euphoria gripped me. I had conquered my fear. Surely that is the greatest victory one can win.

SEVEN

Our cave-dwelling ancestors, like four-footed animals, practised the carnal act from behind. Romans and Greeks did likewise and worse. It was not till the Christian era that couples faced one another; man atop woman in a far more dignified configuration. This manner of copulation is the most effective of all for procreation, which is of course the sole Christian function of such activity. It is the posture, to the exclusion of all others, that is to be assumed in pursuit of such function, by those who fear God, be they layman or missionary; provided they are joined in holy matrimony, one to the other. [Archbishop of Canterbury]

In the morning, a doctor was summoned from the village. He diagnosed my injury as a badly turned ankle. I was to keep off it for a few days and then would require a cane for a week or so. I had no idea that something so minor could be so incapacitating.

I explained to one and all that I had stumbled inadvertently whilst getting out of bed. It seemed a reasonable explanation and was taken as such. Everyone was sympathetic. Everyone actually, save Bettina, who in the process of collecting my clothes for the laundress, eyed me suspiciously. My dress was soiled much more than could be explained by ordinary wear and one stocking was in tatters. I suspect she concluded that I had spent the night out on the moor with a passionate and uncontrollable lover.

I spent the next day in bed reading Trollope. That evening I was visited in my bedchamber by one and all. My recovery was toasted in champagne, whilst I enjoyed an enthusiastic gamahuching from Sir Harry's cunning tongue. Afterwards, taking care not to disturb my immobile ankle, I was fucked thrice, once each by Mr Aziz, Sir Harry, and my hostess, Lady Doris, who wore a most ingenious double-headed dildo – one end in her, the other in me. Pains were taken throughout not to disturb my immobile ankle. Poor Noel Fibbet sat enigmatically through it all, smiling once or twice, knowingly, when he caught my eye. It was obvious he had not yet fulfilled the commitment to deflower his young lady. Nevertheless, he returned later that night to tell me that Deborah, the sweet, virginal target of his lust, was to be a house guest the following week. That done, he proceeded to add his seed to that of his father and the Turk.

The following day, with the swelling down somewhat, I hobbled about on a cane and worked on the manuscript. My trunk arrived from London – a great relief – and I was informed that there were to be house guests over the weekend. That afternoon I was visited by the monthly curse – which was all for the better as I needed the rest.

By Friday morning the ankle swelling disappeared and I found I was favouring my left foot only slightly. With a sigh of relief I dispensed almost simultaneously with both the cane and the uncomfortable cotton batting between my thighs.

At breakfast I was seated next to a charming girl, no older than eighteen. Because Noel was fussing over her like a mother hen, I knew even before we were introduced, that here was the infamous virgin object of his lustful commitment – Miss Deborah MacDill. She was indeed a lovely thing, sporting wide innocent eyes, the complexion of an unplucked peach, and winsome ways – certainly worthy of young Noel's every effort.

The charming Miss MacDill was on school holiday and, along with her aunt, a Mrs Rose Carnaby, would stay through the weekend. Mrs Carnaby was also a welcome addition to our table. An attractive, plumpish woman I took to be in her middle or late thirties, Rose Carnaby seemed to possess not only a friendly, outgoing disposition, but a rather keen wit as well.

After breakfast, I retired to my room to prepare myself for my usual morning ablutions. Wearing a dressing gown and equipped with scented French soap and towel, I crossed the hall to the bathchamber.

The Fanshawe House facility was fitted out with all the necessities, including yet another fine, marble example of Mr Crapper's ingenious invention. 'Twas indeed a most pleasant and modern bathchamber, though, I must add, not quite as modern as my own in London. The lack was piped gas. For not only was illuminating gas a great improvement over candles, it was an equal improvement over coal or wood for heating water for the bath. Only a few houses in London were so equipped, and of course, country houses such as this one had to make do.

I entered to find someone in the bath. I was about to leave when she turned. It was Miss MacDill, submerged from the neck down.

'Ah, Miss Everleigh,' she said smiling.

'Forgive me,' said I. 'The door was unlatched and I assumed no one was here.'

'How careless of me,' said she. 'Would you be good enough to latch it?'

Without a word, I complied. The room was pleasantly steamy and warm from the hot water and the wood fire in the bath boiler.

'The towel . . . you intended to bathe?' Her face was radiant in the warm glow of candlelight.

'Yes I —'

'Well then, why not join me? There's more than enough room for two.'

'Thank you, Miss MacDill.' I considered her invitation most gracious.

'Deborah . . .'

'And you must call me Jenny.'

I felt her eyes as I stepped out of my gown. Gingerly I inserted a toe. The water was delightfully hot. Sighing, I lowered myself gingerly into its aqueous embrace. My eyes closed contentedly. How different from my weekly baths as a child, squatting in the small zinc tub, half filled with tepid water. The tub had been in the kitchen, the air chilled, the soap coarse, brown, and gritty. Bathing then was a necessary chore rather than a luxuriously pleasant experience. Surely it was still the same with most of my fellow Britons. How lucky I was. I slumped down, allowing the water to rise all the way to my chin.

Deborah's smile was beguiling. 'Isn't it lovely?'

'Ah yes, lovely. I look forward to it every day at this time.'

'Every day?'

'Whenever possible, sometimes even twice a day.'

'But bathing is said to be unhealthy when done to excess.'

'Perhaps,' said I, sighing. 'But 'tis heaven, nevertheless.'

'Look how your breasts float – like two pretty islands.'

I glanced down at the phenomenon. Lovely, indeed. 'And yours too.'

'Yes, but yours are nicer than mine . . . fatter.' She was silent for a moment, then, 'May I touch them?'

'Yes, please do,' I said, without thinking further.

She ran a tentative finger across my left breast. I closed my eyes once again, savouring the sensuous warmth, the sound of rippling water. I heard my own sigh of pleasure. Thus encouraged, the young lady leaned forward to cup my breast in her hand. In lyrical voice, she said, 'If you'll stand, I'd be happy to soap you.'

I opened my eyes to gaze into hers. They were wide and of hazel hue, seemingly innocent of guile. I assumed that her gracious offer was equally innocent.

'At school we soap each other all the time,' said she, in husky tones, ''tis most pleasant.'

I rose with some difficulty out of the water. She stood in front of me, brazenly surveying my body. Taking her cue, I did likewise.

Deborah was shorter than I, more sparsely fleshed. Her perfectly formed breasts were teacups to my melons, her curves, though sinuous, less pronounced. Her belly was flat, lacking the slight curvature of my own. I glanced downward at her motte. It was profuse, an ebony nest of fine silk that matched her crowning glory. Staring into my eyes, she lathered the white soap cake in her small, delicate hands. Then, taking my arms, she turned me about till my back was to her. The air raised small chill-bumps on my dampened skin.

Deborah started at my shoulders, massaging gently, working her way down my back. When she reached bottom, the caress became firmer.

There was a pause as I heard the squish of fresh lather being created. I squirmed expectantly. Then her fingers, more tentative now, insinuated themselves between the plump globes. They played like butterfly wings in the secret furrow. Ah, thought I, what have we here? Hardly the innocent, tentative activity of a naive virgin!

The soapy caress sent an exquisite shudder through my body. Sensing my reaction, her fingers grew bolder, more insistent, massaging the cleansing froth into sensitive flesh. 'Twas obvious I had been mistaken about the now vivacious Miss Deborah MacDill. I felt my bottom begin to move in small lustful rotations.

'We learn in school that one must be clean everywhere.' Her fingers, in counterpoint to the increasing motion of my bum, played between my buttocks.

'Yes,' said I, 'I'm a firm believer in education.'

'And we must not forget that cleanliness in next to Godliness.'

'How true,' said I.

'Everywhere,' said she.

'Everywhere, indeed,' said I.

Slowly, excruciatingly, her hand slithered under – between my thighs – to cup an awakening mount.

'Twas unseemly activity, though I, for a virgin. But enough conjecture. There would be time for that, later . . .

'Lovely,' she whispered. 'So lovely.' A moan of rapture escaped my lips as a bold, exploring digit searched out the base of my clitoris. I placed my hand on hers, caressing it as she was caressing me.

Then, pressing her body against my back, she reached around with her free hand to soap and pleasure my belly, my breasts; draining me of everything but pleasure. My legs weakened, my breath grew short. She frigged me slowly at first but as my cuntal juices combined in a voluptuous infusion with the soapsuds, the pace increased – faster and faster with ever-increasing pressure until nothing else existed except that secret part – the lascivious centre of my being.

Deborah seemed to sense that she was just moments from fetching me. She withdrew her hand, turned me to her. Her breasts pressed against me, just below my own. I stooped slightly to bring all four rotundities into intimate contact. Our nipples kissed. Our wet bodies, slippery with soap, slithered one against the other, writhing in time to inaudible music – belly to belly, flesh to flesh.

She caressed my face, licked my lips. 'Lovely,' she repeated, her voice pitched low with passion. She fucked my mouth with a tongue that seemed a miniature, stiffened cock. She sucked on it as we pressed even closer together.

My leg, of its own volition, passed between hers. We rode each other's thighs with twitching pussies. Deborah moaned into my mouth as the delicious tension grew like a giant bubble.

As it burst, she arched in rapturous contractions, squealing stridently. 'Fuck, spunk, cunt!' Then, in a sweet, husky whisper: 'Jenny . . .'

Every part of my body vibrated in sustained harmony, a rapturous minor chord. I heard a voice —my own — call out, 'Deborah . . . Deborah!'

EIGHT

The horror which the bride had expressed was, as Mrs Carbuncle well knew, no mock feeling, no pretence of antipathy. She tried to think of it, and to realize what might in truth be the girl's action and ultimate fate when she should find herself in the power of this man whom she so hated. But had not other girls done the same thing, and lived through it all, and become fat, indifferent, and fond of the world? It's only the first step that signifies. [Anthony Trollope]

'I simply have to talk to someone,' said Deborah. 'A friend.'

It was late at night. She had knocked quietly on my door just as I was falling asleep. She wore a silk dressing gown, her hair up under a pink lace bed cap.

She sighed and said, 'It's about Noel Fibbit . . .'

'A lover's quarrel?'

'No, that's just it.' Seating herself next to me, she looked down forlornly at her feet. 'We're hardly lovers.'

I placed a sympathetic hand on hers. 'I understand.'

'You do?'

'Yes,' said I, squeezing her hand and placing an arm around her shoulders. 'He thinks you are an innocent virgin and you are not.'

She stood abruptly to stare at me as if I were a witch. 'How could you possibly know?'

'I'm quite experienced with that sort of thing.'

An expression of horror darkened her face. 'One can tell just by looking at me . . . I knew that would be so . . . I just knew it!' Tears formed in her eyes; she sobbed.

'No, Deborah,' said I, once again reaching out to take her hand.

'I'm only eighteen and I'm ruined.'

'You're far from ruined. You've only just begun. As for your late virginity, good riddance. After eighteen it becomes a preoccupation and then a chronic disease. And it will cheer you to know that one cannot tell by looking at you.'

'Truly?'

'Truly,' said I. 'On seeing you for the first time, one is struck immediately by your apparent innocence, your obvious chastity. That's why this morning in the tub I was surprised to realize that such might not be the case; though I must say the experience was lovely.'

'Oh yes, Jenny, indeed it was.' She sat on the bed again. 'But then, how could you know?'

'It might not seem so to you, dear Deborah, but not very long ago, I too was a virgin, and I too played sensuous little games. But, as are most chaste maidens, I was always the "victim" never the aggressor as you were this morning. And your language . . . words that could only have been learned from a man.' I smiled at her. 'Or did your apprenticeship include more than just a single masculine instructor?'

She blushed. 'There have been three.'

'When was the first?'

'Two months ago — two months and four days. An older gentleman.'

'An excellent choice.'

'The others were boys but Mr Plimber, who is a writer of poetry, did it to me eleven times in three days. He taught me everything.'

'Not everything, Deborah.'

'You mean there is more?'

65

'There's always more; one never stops learning. That's the joy of it.'

She fell back on the bed to stare at the ceiling. 'You make my head spin!'

'So,' said I, 'we come to the matter in hand.'

'Yes, Noel, the poor dear, has been longing to deflower me.'

'Indeed he has,' said I. 'And men don't like being fooled. 'Twould be a devastating shock to him to find you've been previously plucked.'

Even as I spoke, a plan began to formulate itself in mind. I ran my hand lightly down the silk-sheathed length of her body.

'What am I to do, dear Jenny?'

'Have no fear,' said I softly, my mouth just inches from hers. 'I have a plan . . . a foolproof plan.'

'Oh, Jenny,' said she, throwing her arms around me. 'I knew I could count on you!'

She was a silly girl with what seemed to me to be a trivial problem. I would solve it for her and, in the process, recruit a devoted ally.

She arched her body, raising her hips off the bed to aid me in removing her gown. 'Oh, do tell me all about it, Jenny! What are we going to do?'

'Later . . .'

'Are you certain your plan will work?'

'I promise, have no fear.'

She was silent for a while before speaking softly into my mouth. 'This time,' said she, 'it is you who will be the aggressor and I the passive one – the victim.'

'Spoken like a true virgin,' said I.

After Deborah MacDill returned to her own room. I ventured once again into the hidden passageways beyond my fireplace. It was to be a long night of exploration between the walls.

Equipped with extra candles and sulphur matches, I

roamed freely throughout a rabbit's warren of passageways, climbing and descending ladders between floors, keeping track of junctions, learning my way about. It was gratifying to find that the dark, secret halls of Fanshawe House no longer held terror for me; nor did those harmless creatures rustling and squealing in the dark just beyond the range of my candle.

I located seventeen more peepholes. Near each was an access lever to activate a secret entrance. Eleven of the peepholes opened into bedrooms. The other seven included the study, the morning room, the entrance hall, the kitchen, the main lounge, an empty room in the unused wing, and a room of such evil aspect that for minutes it defied all logical conjecture as to its function. It, like the kitchen, was below-stairs; a very large chamber, sporting tiled floors and walls. Most unusual, it contained an oval pool of water the diameter of which I reckoned to be roughly twenty-five feet. There were strange devices scattered about, some mounted on the floor and walls, others suspended from the ceiling. Was it, I wondered, some sort of torture chamber?

Roaming through the dark but increasingly familiar passageways was fast becoming a happy part of one of my favourite activities: voyeurism. Nothing could be hidden from me.

Noel Fibbit lay sprawled across his bed, in his left hand a small book, in his right his erect pego. He stroked slowly, pausing every now and again to turn a page. From my vantage point of but a few feet away, I could make out, embossed in gold leaf on a Moroccon spine, the title: *Autobiography of a Flea — Book III.*

Deborah MacDill lay sleeping in a flow of moonlight filtering through diaphanous drapes. Hardly the sleep of an innocent, her tossings and turnings were orchestrated by squeals and grunts and sharp little ladylike snores. I suspected her dream involved an amorous young Noel Fibbit, who even now, in real life, might be climaxing explosively to tales of a wondrously erotic flea.

Deborah's aunt, Mrs Rose Carnaby, sat in an armchair, reading avidly by the light of a few candles. I was pleased to find she shared my taste for Trollope and looked forward to an eventual literary discussion.

Mr Aziz was also asleep, though much more deeply so than the agitated Miss MacDill. 'Twas clear that he had since experienced the nightly, conjugal visit of a benevolently oral Bettina.

The peephole opening into the Fibbit bedchamber was placed high on the wall, but a convenient step provided access to it. Lady Doris, sporting a voluminous nightdress, lay, propped up by innumerable pillows, on a canopied bed. Sir Harry in a bright red flannel nightgown and nightcap sat before a small French desk. I was surprised to see a very unmaidlike Bettina in lacy, pink silk nightclothes, pacing back and forth across the room. She seemed agitated.

Lady Doris said, 'But you can't keep changing my dear.'

'Why can't I?' Bettina halted in her tracks, turned to Lady Doris. 'I'm tired of being Bettina – of being a maid.'

'I've grown quite fond of you as Bettina,' said Lady Doris. 'You've made an excellent maid. 'Tis a far better impersonation than last year's example of Russian aristocracy. You might recall that evening in Biarritz – the Grand Duke Alexis and his party. The dinner was an absolute embarrassment for all of us! Awful!'

'And you, dear Mother, might recall that neither yourself, the Grand Duke, nor I was the least bit embarrassed in his big bed later that very night.'

'Beside the point,' said Sir Harry. 'The fact is, you couldn't speak the language and your accent sounded more Gallic than Russian – terrible!'

'I did the best I could.'

'You needn't have done it at all,' said Sir Harry. 'These childlike masquerades are solely your idea, and your mother and I reserve the right to criticize them.'

'They are not masquerades, Father, I'm an actress!'

'And I'm Queen of the May.'

'Who is it you want to be this time?' said Lady Doris.

'I want to be French – an elegant French lady.'

'Good Lord!' said Sir Harry. 'That will indeed be a trial to us all.'

'Please?'

'Well, you speak the language,' said Lady Doris. 'I'll give you that.'

'I speak it well. And as for accent – I've been practising. Just listen.'

Before my eyes 'Bettina' altered her posture. At once she became looser, her body seemingly softer, her shoulders slumped forward, her chin raised up. If 'Bettina' had been playing to the balcony, the character I now observed through my peephole was playing to the orchestra. As she spoke, I listened in amazement to an accent, authentically and heavily French.

'My name is Mademoiselle Babette Chartreuse,' said she, in lyrical frenchified tones, almost an octave lower than the Cockney Bettina. 'I am a beautiful and mysterious French woman from Paris and I've grown to despise that horrid maid Bettina. Off with her head!'

'Bravo!' shouted Lady Doris.

'Thank you, Mother.'

'How thinks you, Harry?' said Lady Doris.

His tone was reluctant. 'Quite good.'

'Thank you.'

'But those who know Bettina the maid will see through it.'

'No, Father, even you will not recognize me.' She loosened some pins and then, to my surprise, removed, with a sweeping gesture, a blond wig she was wearing. 'Babette will be crowned with my very own dark hair. I will make my cheekbones more prominent and will kohl my eyes. Everything will be different.'

'But how will we explain the absence of Bettina?' said Sir Harry.

69

Bettina-Babette smiled. 'We will simply say that she had to return to London for a while to look after her ailing mum.'

'Poor Mr Aziz will go sleepless without your nightly ministrations,' said Lady Doris.

'Well then, Mother, perhaps you might take over that particular chore.'

'I think, my dear,' said Lady Doris, 'that the new Babette might be more suited to the task.'

Sir Harry's voice took on the stern qualities of a school-master. 'One doesn't rid oneself of a responsibility merely by changing one's identity.'

'I thought one did . . .'

'Let's not all get into a snit now,' said Lady Doris.

'May I be Mademoiselle Babette Chartreuse?'

'It's up to your father.'

'Daddy, please.' She took his hand in hers. ''Twill be a real giggle for all of us – the best one yet.'

'You are a spoiled child,' said Sir Harry.

'I'm not a child.' Folding her arms, she locked both his hands against her breasts. 'Please? 'Just think how lovely it will be to have a deliciously randy French lady toddling about the house.'

A smile broke through the mock severity darkening his face. 'You and your mother always manage to have your way with me.'

'Hurrah!' Wiggling her hips joyfully, she pulled Sir Harry tight against her. 'Oh, thank you, Father!'

'Enough of that,' said Sir Harry, turning her about to deliver a slap to her bottom. ''Tis late and a full night's sleep is called for. Tomorrow our guests arrive.'

'Oh Harry, she only wants to thank you with a little fuck,' said Lady Doris, turning to her daughter. 'Don't you, my dear?'

'A quick fuck, to be sure.'

'Get you to your room, young lady,' said Sir Harry. 'When next we fuck, you will be Mademoiselle Babette Chartreuse!'

70

Between the walls, I sank to the floor in amazement. The Fibbit family was indeed mad!

Though I could no longer see them, their voices remained audible through the wooden partition. After an interminably long expression of gratitude and a profusion of 'good nights,' Bettina – soon to be Babette – was gone.

'A lovely girl, our daughter,' said Lady Doris.

'She's headstrong, wilful, shrewd, bold, quick, and devious,' said Sir Harry. 'Attributes that will make her a magnificent woman if ever she grows up and develops moderation and stability.'

'Who would have dreamed that an adopted daughter would grow to be so like her parents?'

''S truth,' said Sir Harry.

'Perhaps you're too hard on her.'

'No harder than on Noel, our natural son. I play no favourites.'

Once again I stood to place my eye to the peephole. Sir Harry was in bed, his back to Lady Doris.

'You speak to our children of commitment and responsibility,' said Lady Doris, placing a hand on his shoulder.

'Yet what of your own conjugal duties and obligations? 'Tis almost twenty-four hours since I last experienced them.'

'I must be excused from such considerations tonight, madam. I'm quite exhausted.'

'Ah, then may I take it that my husband is finally suffering the disabilities of advanced age?'

'No, you may not. Even a young boy would feel the effects of four hours in the arms of Mrs Carnaby.'

'She sounds interesting.'

'*Insatiable* would be a more accurate term.'

'Poor Harry.'

'Indeed.'

'Perhaps you are not getting enough exercise.'

'More than enough, thank you.'

'Then not enough carrots and apples.'

'I'm sick of both.'

'Dr Hochenbusch will be here tomorrow, perhaps he can recommend something else.'

'One can only hope so. But it is more important that he have with him the Suez shares from Zurich.'

What, I wondered, was their meaning? Exercise, carrots, apples, as prescribed by a Dr Hochenbusch? The context was indeed a strange one. Exercise at what? Was this a kind of recipe for a magical or medical elixir for impotency? As I mulled it over in my mind, two other words that had been uttered by Sir Harry stopped me short. *Suez shares!*

In a state of sudden excitement, I turned away from the peephole. The game, I realized, was afoot! Edward had been right. Sir Harry Fibbit was indeed a traitor to his country! And, thought I, my pulse racing, little Jenny Everleigh was in an ideal position to thwart his awful villainy. God save the Queen!

I started back toward my bedroom when I realized that there was a duty still to perform. Though its importance paled when compared to my larger duty, a promise was a promise. For this purpose it was required I use the secret kitchen entrance.

Once there, in order to ensure that the coast was clear, I peered through the peephole. I was greeted with the sight of the enigmatic butler Starns seated at a rough-hewn kitchen table in the light of a single candle, attacking what was left of a very large trifle that had been served at dinner that very evening.

I stilled my agitated impatience with the thought that he would not be long at his feast; probably only five, or at most, ten minutes more. Then, just as I was about to lower myself to a seated position on the floor where I could wait him out in relative comfort, a dim apparition appeared behind him. It took a moment for it to resolve itself into the figure of a young girl . . . the scullery maid.

72

She cleared her throat politely, causing Starns to turn to her. 'I'm sorry, Mr Starns,' said she. 'I heard someone rummaging about and —'

'That's all right, Clara,' said he pleasantly. 'Would you care for a bit of trifle?'

'Thank you all the same but I've already had some for my supper.' Her voice carried the musical accents of heavy Cockney. 'Can I get you something else, Mr Starns?'

'No thank you.' With a fastidious gesture he touched napkin to lip. 'Come into the light, child, where I can see you.'

She took a tentative step forward. She wore a faded, hand-me-down nightgown, on her head a cheap white cotton bed cap. A few unkempt locks of red hair peeped from under it.

'Come closer, Clara.'

She took another step. Her wide eyes gleamed in the candlelight.

'You are a pretty little thing, aren't you?'

'Oh no sir . . .' She turned her head away, obviously blushing.

'How old are you, Clara?'

'Fifteen. I think,' she said. 'But perhaps seventeen. I'm not rightly sure.' Blinking rapidly, she stared at his extended hand, then backed off a step. 'But now I think it best that I be getting back to my bed if it's all the same to you, Mr Starns.'

'Come here where I can see you better.'

'Oh, I couldn't . . .'

'Take my hand, dear girl.'

'Oh sir.'

'I'm not going to hurt you.' He extended both his hands to her. She stepped forward shyly. He grasped her wrists, pulling her toward him.

'I must go to bed now, Mr Starns, sir.'

'Well then, kiss us good night.'

'Oh sir!' She pointed a vain attempt to pull away from

73

him. From my vantage point, it seemed but halfhearted. 'Oh sir!'

'Now give us that kiss.' He put his arm about her waist, drawing her closer.

'Oh sir!'

'Let's have it, dear Clara – your lips.'

'Oh no sir . . . I mean, toward what end?'

'Towards your end of course.'

'Oh sir!'

'A kiss will do you no harm Clara, and 'twill please me greatly.'

'I can't begin to imagine why.'

'I like you. I've always thought you a pretty little thing.'

'You have?'

'Since you first arrived in this house a month ago.'

'Why would you, sir, a butler – notice the likes of me?'

'It is my function to take note of everything in this house.' He placed both hands on her waist, squeezing it till the fingers met. 'For example, you have such a tiny waist that no corset is required to hold it in, a rare and natural beauty that the real ladies of this household would rightly envy.'

'Oh, Mr Starns, how can you utter such lewd things!'

I peered through my peephole, praying impatiently they get on with it so that I might go on about my business. The outcome was, of course, inevitable. The only question was one of time.

'A kiss, dear girl, a simple kiss for an admirer.'

'You're just using words to turn an innocent girl's head.'

'A single, friendly meeting of our lips will be enough to comfort me through the long night.' Releasing a drawn-out sigh, he pulled her into his lap.

'Heavens! Let me up! Cook would be beside herself if she saw us!'

'But how will she see us? At this very moment, Mrs Henry's in her room, beyond the pantry, sound asleep. An earthquake wouldn't awaken her, much less a single kiss.'

'But she's diabolical, she is. She has a mystical way of knowing about every bleeding thing that happens in her kitchen.'

'It matters not, for tomorrow I will put in a word for you.'

'You will?'

'Yes, dear girl. Cook takes great stock in my advice.'

'What will you tell her?'

'I will tell her that if she wishes, she may hire another scullery girl and raise you to kitchen maid. She will certainly have nothing against another assistant — and Bob's your uncle. Two birds with one stone, as they say.'

'Oh, Mr Starns, how kind of you! Just think of it! I'll wear a uniform and sleep in a real room.'

'Now a kiss to seal the bargain, dear Clara.'

'Well then, if it's just the one kiss. I must be up at dawn to peel potatoes and clean the fish and—'

He pulled her to him, pressed his lips to hers. I was pleased to note that they were finally getting on with it.

Starns broke off the kiss abruptly. With his hands grasping her shoulders, he said, 'Dear girl, you are not, I take it, affected with lockjaw?'

'Of course not,' she said, vexation colouring her words. 'I'm a clean girl! Mrs Henry insists the kitchen staff all bath once a week whether needed or not.'

'And you have a tongue?'

'Of course!' She stuck it out.

'And you are capable of closing your eyes?'

'Yes but—'

'Then if you come equipped with all those facilities, why is it that to kiss you is akin to kissing a wall?'

'I'm sorry. Mr Starns, sir,' said Clara, her voice stiff with indignation. 'But 'twas your idea, not mine, I assure you!'

He held her tightly as she attempted to stand up. 'I'll teach you. 'Tis simple, once one gets the hang of it.' He brought his face close to hers. 'Don't, dear Clara, pucker your lips as if I were your aunt, but open them to me —

slightly – enough so that my tongue may gain entrance. Then, when you feel it in your mouth, touch it with your own; engage it in a gentle duel of love. And my lips will also be parted and open to your own lingual invasion. You will suck my tongue as I suck yours. And it is best to keep one's eyes closed.'

'Why, Mr Starns?'

'So that one's feelings may be concentrated on the matter at hand.' Once again the butler pressed his lips to those of the serving girl. My hopes for a speedy conclusion were raised as this time the kiss seemed a more successful one. Clara's arms, which till now had been hanging limp by her side, were now raised, bent at the elbow, fists clenched. A soft, muffled moan escaped her busy lips. It was a long, drawn-out kiss that went on for minutes.

Finally they parted. Clara's eyes remained shut as in a small voice she said, 'And now you've had your kiss, Mr Starns, it is time I went to my bed.' She squirmed about on Starns lap in a sham attempt to break loose. One of his hands went to her breast. He cupped it delicately.

'Oh sir!' She grasped his wrist.

'Ah, delightful . . . such pretty, plump little breasts you have . . . so firm and young. Are you a virgin, Clara?'

Her eyes shot open. 'Oh please Mr Starns, how can you ask such an improper question of a poor, innocent scullery maid.'

'Are you, my sweet?'

Except for a sharp intake of breath, she was silent as the butler tweaked a nipple through the thin material of her bed gown. Then, quite suddenly, she exhaled a deep sigh and placed her arms around his neck. Her head dropped to his shoulder.

'Can we kiss again, Mr Starns . . . like before?'

'In a moment, my sweet. But first my question must be answered.' In a flash, his hand was under her skirt. She shot up in his lap, grasped his arm.

'Oh, sir! What are you doing!'

I observed the movement of his invisible hand beneath the fabric, where the apex of her thighs would be: a lascivious sight, despite my impatience.

'Ah, it's a juicy little thing.'

'Oh sir!' She attempted to cross her legs.

'Now hold still.'

'Oh sir!'

'Feel how easily my finger slips in, dear Clara.'

'Ohhh sirrr . . .'

'All the way, my dear . . . to the final knuckle . . . there . . . Ah, you're not a virgin after all.'

Clara slumped in his arms, pressed her lips to his for another extended kiss. I felt my own quim warming up, salivating as I watched the increasingly rapid movement beneath her skirt. 'Twas as if a small, secret animal was scurrying about under the cloth!

Stirred by what I saw before me, my hand, as if by its own volition, descended into the juncture of my own thighs, pressing tightly. Even through my clothing my quim felt soft to the touch, lubricated, awakened by my peephole view of what promised to be a most lascivious congress.

As they kissed, Starns manoeuvred Clara's bottom till it rested on his knees. Thus with his lap unoccupied, he used his free hand to unfasten the buttons on his trousers. After a good deal of fumbling, his prick, fully erected, emerged. It stood, proud and unencumbered, like a flagstaff awaiting the hoisting of a victory banner.

With my eyes glued to the opening. I watched as Starns frigged himself with a slow and purposeful stroke. That indulgence, however was but brief. There was a strategic task of higher priority awaiting him. One must undertake first things first, as they say. Releasing the turgid member, his clever hand strayed to the back of Clara's nightdress and proceded to unfasten the hooks. I admired his adroitness. To succeed single-handed at such a task required both experience and dexterity. (Few men possess, in this day and age, a talent for undressing women.) In the meanwhile, his other hand continued its tactical diversion beneath Clara's skirt.

In the darkness of my secure blind, I raised my own skirt and proceeded, with delicate fingers but firm resolve, to emulate the digital machinations of the randy butler. My fingers, like his, strolled happily in an ambrosial garden. I was sopping, even, as must be, the coy scullery maid. Was her mons veneris as plump and voluptuous as mine? Were the pads of sweet moist flesh as firm and elastic? Was her clitoris as well proportioned, as responsive? Was its base as thick and as exquisitely sensitive?

Probably not. Few women approach such aesthetic cuntal perfection. I mean not to be immodest, but truth is truth. I take extraordinary pride in the beauteous organ between my thighs, lavishing as much attention on it as I do on my complexion. One must, you know. I mean, it is only proper to take good care of that which provides a far greater degree of joy and pleasure than any other part of one's body. I trim and shape the hair as if it were a second coif. I douche daily with oil of cloves and apply, externally, a secret unguent given to me by chief houris of Tewfik Pasha's Egyptian harem. Treat it right and it will treat you right is my motto. Most women of my acquaintance would be shocked to hear me speaking in this manner. In fact, many of them are as ignorant about their own intimate geography as they are about Siam's. For example, in order to forestall unwanted pregnancies, they douche with such horrid corrosive solutions as mercuric-cyanide or suphate of zinc. I have long since ceased doing so on the assumption that it is self-destructive to put anything in one's vagina that one would hesitate, for whatever reason, to put into one's mouth. Instead, I make use of a cunning device called a 'French cup.' Worn internally and anchored securely, it is comprised of a metal ring with india rubber stretched across it. It stands guard over the uterus and is quite undetectable. Of course during 'unripe' days no such protection is needed. ('French cups' are available at a bookshop in Mayfair, but only if one presents 'respectable' references.)

Carried away momentarily by the joys of masturbation, I had allowed my eye to stray from the peephole. I returned eagerly to it to note that the top part of Clara's nightgown had dropped, exposing a perfectly matched pair of adorable breasts. With the now half-naked scullery maid still balanced on his knees, Starns was paying lingual homage to an erect pink nipple. The scullery maid's head was thrown back, her eyes closed, her breathing heavy and laced with sweet little whimpers. As if not entirely in her control, her hips were circumnavigating, slowly and unevenly, about the fulcrum of the butler's hidden machinations.

Even as I watched, Starns grasped her hand to bring it in contact with his naked pego. It took a moment for her to realize the nature of the object. Her body stiffened. She pulled her hand away as if it had been in contact with a hot coal. Her eyes opened abruptly.

'Oh, sir!' She shot erect and it was all Starns could do to keep her falling to the floor.

''Tis only my cock, dear girl,' said he. 'Not, I assure you, some horrid, fanged, bloodthirsty beastie that might bite you.'

'But—'

'Surely, dear girl, you have in the past come into contact with the instrument in question. My forefinger has indicated at least that and perhaps more . . . much more.'

'What must you think of me! Oh heavens.'

'Well . . . until just a moment ago, I was sucking your tit and my hand was buried in your pussy and I was in the process, actually, of thinking quite highly of you.'

'How can you mouth such lewd words in front of a lady?'

He stood, unceremoniously dumping her onto the floor. She lay there, arms and legs outstretched as he loomed over her, his erect penis pointing into the darkness.

'You are no more a lady than I, my dear, am a gentleman.

79

In fact real ladies and gentlemen speak thusly all the time. But that is beside the point. The real point is that you are female and I male. Happenstance or God or fate has created an erotic propinquity. But enough is quite enough. Do we or do we not fuck? If you say not, I will detain you no longer from your miserable pallet. And have no fear, I am, dear Clara, a seducer, not a rapist . . . though, come to think of it, I'm not certain which of the two you would prefer.'

'I've never heard such talk.'

'No doubt,' said Starns, grasping his cock. Nevertheless, the decision is yours.'

She sat on the floor, staring up at the granitic prick. She seemed dazed.

'Well?'

She was quiet for a long moment. Then in a small voice, she said, 'If I leave, will you kiss me good night again?'

'Indeed.'

He helped her to her feet. Keeping his distance, he placed an innocent peck of a kiss on her cheek then stepped back. She stood, confused, seemingly helpless, holding her night-gown in place.

'Good night, Clara.' He turned away and, without looking back, paced the distance with great dignity to the kitchen door.

'Oh sir!' In a trice she reached him, turned him about. He grasped her hips as she threw herself against his body.

There followed yet another kiss that seemed to last an eternity. In the process she reached down to grasp his cock with what seemed a sure and experienced hand.

Ah, thought I, the moment of literal truth has arrived! I ran a gentle finger back and forth, first a bare millimetre to the right, and then a millimetre to the left of my clitoris, barely touching it. The effect was an exquisite sensation that passed through my body to the back of my neck, my breasts, and the base of my spine.

With lips connected, they fell to the cold, stone floor;

Starns on his back, Clara, cock in hand, astride. For a few moments, she frigged him vigorously. Then with a deep moan, she broke off the kiss and raised herself to a squatting position.

With a surprising facility, she pulled Starns's trousers and underdrawers to his knees. Then, sighting down the length of the butler's body, she aligned herself, Slowly she lowered her hips. Starns's cock was at the portal. Then, before my eyes, its plump, purple helmet entered the luscious sanctuary.

I placed a thumb at the base of my clitoris whilst two fingers made their way in and upward to contact the secret, internal spot known to just a few fortunate women. Thusly, I frigged as Clara's determined cunt swallowed Starns's cock.

When she had it all, she became as a wild Hungarian Hussar galloping to the charge!

'Oh sir!'

'Fuck, Clara, my sweet . . . fuck!' He reached up with both hands to pinch her nipples.

'Oh please don't speak so!' Her hips thrust up and down as if animated by an ingenious clockwork.

Frigging faster and faster, I thrilled to the sound of female arseflesh impacting male thighflesh: to the rhythmic squishing sound of joyful fuckery! Now both of my hands were involved in lustful pursuits. The finger of one pinched my clitoris whilst the thumb massaged its oiled surface. With the other, I finger-fucked, using three digits in an attempt to simulate a thrusting cock. 'Twas heavenly! My eyes were glued to the cunting and un-cunting of the butler's magnificent tool as the scullery maid's milk-white arse undulated wildly!

'Oh sir, what you're doing to me!'

'I'm doing nothing, Clara,' said Starns, his voice strained with passion. 'I'm merely laying here . . .

'Oh sir!'

'Fuck me, dear girl!'

'I'm going to spend!'

'Fuck! Fuck! Take my cock all the way up! Frig it with your pussy!'

'Ah Mr Starns.'

'Fuck! Cunt! Cock! Arsehole! Spunk!'

'Oh sir!'

'Fuck it, Clara!'

'I'm spending!'

'I'm shooting in you! Feel it! Take it all!'

She sat on his groin, her eyes clamped shut. Manly groans and feminine squeals combined in a lascivious orchestration of lust as her body trembled uncontrollably.

Finally they were quiet. It was then that my furious masturbation resulted in my own orgasm. I sighed, groaned aloud as the tension built to fruition.

A few moments later I opened my eyes. Starns, weighted down beneath the recumbent chambermaid, was staring directly at my peephole. Had he heard me? Worse – had he seen my single glaring eye? My heart, still racing from recent exertions, was pounding fearfully. For an instant I thought he might hear its beating. I struggled to calm myself. Surely it was impossible to notice the peephole in the darkness at my end of the kitchen. He was simply reacting to an unexplained noise . . . the sound of a woman in the throes of passion. But then why was he staring directly into my peephole? Why were his eyes staring directly into mine even though he could not see it? Could he know of the secret passageways? I steeled myself and prepared to bolt if he approached the wall.

Clara diverted his attention by assuming a sitting position on his chest. 'I'm so ashamed. Mr Starns . . . you must think me an awful girl. But please don't tell anyone. I mean, I've never done anything like this before and I –'

Mr Starns, rose up abruptly, lifting her to her feet. He slapped her on the rump. 'Go to bed and I will do likewise and no one will ever be the wiser.'

'Will you put in a word for me with Mrs Henry as you promised?'

'Yes.'

'And what,' said she, 'if I am with child?'

'That would be quite unwise of you, dear girl.'

'Can we do it again?'

'Perhaps.'

'When?'

'Good night, Clara.'

'Good night, sir.' She turned from him reluctantly and made her way into the dimness beyond the candlelight. She turned once, as if to say something, then changing her mind, she disappeared into the service hall.

Mr Starns breathed a sigh of relief, then glancing once in the direction of my peephole, left the kitchen.

Suspecting that he might be lying in wait. I allowed a half hour to go by before emerging cautiously into the kitchen through a hinged portion of the stone wall.

My plan to aid Miss MacDill revolved around two substances to be found only belowstairs. I located the first of these, powered alum, in one of the larder cabinets. Most large households keep it on hand to use as an insecticide or for making glue or fixing dyes. (My ex-benefactress, Madam Kooshay, used alum in a mixture with white of egg, powdered eggshell, borax, poppy seeds, and water as a cosmetic mask.) But there was yet another function I had in mind.

My second requirement could be satisfied with a small amount of blood from a side of beef hanging in the cold room. But first, it was necessary for me to return, via the walls, to the Fibbit bedchamber.

I entered through a panel, hidden adroitly in a wall of wood panelling. Sir Harry and Lady Doris were snoring an inharmonious duet that I disturbed not at all. My sole interest was to acquire a perfume vial. Thus equipped with one from Lady Doris's dressing table. I returned belowstairs where I replaced the perfume with about a quarter ounce of cow's blood.

Dawn found me back in my own room, euphoric with a

sense of power. I was a phantom, able now to move about freely in total secret, to see without being seen, to enter and leave any one of eighteen rooms without anybody being aware that I had even left my own. No spy could ask for more.

I awoke sometime after noon.

NINE

Soixante-neuf: now there indeed, is a magical, mystical number! [Lillie Langtree]

I awoke in time to join the recently arrived guests for luncheon. Seated amongst them was a gentleman with whom, almost two years earlier in London, I had spent a rather delicious evening. As I approached he rose to his feet with the other gentlemen, a puzzled frown on his face. It was soon displaced by a bright flash of recognition.

'By George, it's Jenny!'

'Mr Stubbs,' said I. 'What a lovely surprise!'

Smiling broadly, he took my hand. 'How marvellous! You've grown into a woman since I last saw you.'

'That was at least partially due to you, dear Mr Stubbs.'

'My darling Jenny, you flatter me.' He kissed my hand 'And a lady in the bargain,' he said, quietly, with a sly wink.

He was referring, of course to the upper-class accent I had acquired since our tête-à-tête. Smiling back, I said, 'That too reflects the beneficial results of education and 'twas bestowed on me by yet another kind gentleman.'

Mr Stubbs turned to introduce me to the other house guests. The first of these was Babette Chartreuse. Wonder of wonders! She bore not the least resemblance to the 'late' Bettina! Even seated, she looked taller, somehow slimmer, than her predecessor. (I have always valued the advantages of good posture.) Her accent was perfect — even more musically French than that which she had demonstrated to her parents the previous night.

Next to Mademoiselle Chartreuse was seated Dr Josef Hochenbusch. He was a giant of a man, equally impressive in both breadth and height. The middle-aged doctor towered well over six feet with shoulders that seemed more appropriate to an ox than to a human being. He seemed at first glance to be bloated with fat, but as I was to find later, the excessive bulk under his sombre clothing consisted exclusively of taut muscle. He looked, thought I, very unusual for a doctor. Men of medicine, in my experience, have all been bearded, balding, squat, and portly. Dr Hochenbusch was none of these. He sported a monocle, a full head of grey hair, and despite his bulk, a stiff and formal bearing. Though my experience in such matters was, at the time, somewhat limited, the good doctor seemed in manner and comportment to be more Prussian than Swiss, more military than medical.*

As Dr Hochenbusch took my hand I could not help speculating on a secret vision of this masculine hulk lying atop a woman. Surely, she would be lost under the tonnage: totally invisible, creating the illusion of the Swiss behemoth mating without benefit of a partner. Our congregation included yet another foreigner: Mr Samuel Smith, a handsome American who seemed a slim and elegant elm next to Dr Hochenbusch's massive oak. His hair was light brown, almost blond, and like the rest of him was charmingly shaggy. Much in the way of the few other Americans I had met previously, he affected a most peculiar manner of speech, a kind of drawl that somehow seemed, at the same time, to be both relaxed and animated.

As I assumed my seat at the long table Lady Doris turned to me to say. 'You must tell us all about your previous association with Mr Stubbs. The little I heard sounds positively delicious.'

* In fairness I must add that perhaps such conjecture on my part might have been a prejudice engendered by what I had learned the night before of his diabolical mission.

'Yes, Miss Everleigh,' said Mademoiselle Chartreuse, 'please do.'

I flushed. 'I believe that to be Mr Stubbs's prerogative.'

''Tis hardly fit for luncheon conversation,' said Mr Stubbs.

'In that case we'll discuss it at dinner,' said Lady Doris.

'Sounds marvellously randy,' said Mrs Carnaby, staring first at Mr Stubbs, then at myself over the top of her wineglass. 'But perhaps it best wait till we all become better acquainted.'

I smiled at her appreciatively. The rest of our table talk consisted of the usual inconsequential chitchat. Mr Smith sat on my left and managed most of his lunch with one hand whilst the other advanced, between soup and dessert, from my knee to the inside of my thigh. I was about to leave the table when I recalled the Prince of Wales's reference to an American consortium. It occurred to me that Mr Smith might also be delivering share certificates. The game was indeed afoot! I decided to stay awhile, just long enough to allow him to complete his secret exploration.

Then, flashing a significant glance at Deborah, I rose from the table. She nodded. Five minutes later, breathless with expectation, she knocked at my bedroom door.

'Alum,' said I, handing her a small envelope. 'I assume that the best method is to dissolve it in warm water to use as a douche.'

'What will it do?' said she nervously.

'It will make you tight, like the virgin you're supposed to be.'

'Heavens . . .'

'But you must use it within an hour or so before the event.'

'All of it?'

'Yes, the more the better. You must make the rascal work for his pleasure.'

'Will it hurt?'

'Perhaps.'

'Well, it's supposed to, I guess.'

'And this,' said I, handing her the perfume vial, 'contains a small amount of blood – have no fear, it's beef blood. You are to hide it somewhere within reach. Afterwards, while he is catching his breath, sprinkle it on the sheets. Men love to gloat over the results of their prowess.'

'Oh Jenny, you are a marvel!'

'Remember, no more than an hour, two at the most.' I took her hand. 'Think of yourself as an innocent bride. And for heaven's sake, demonstrate neither knowledge nor aggression.'

'But then how will I get him to come to me during that span of time?'

'I'll arrange that,' said I. 'Let us say four o'clock this afternoon in your room.'

'Oh Jenny, I can hardly wait!' She threw her arms about me. 'What a glorious way to spend the tea time . . . I'll be in bed when he opens the door . . . I'll be naked . . . and then –'

'No, Deborah,' said I. 'Virgins are never naked. You must be fully clothed – demure – and after you swoon from his kisses, you must leave it to him to undress you.'

'Yes, yes, it sounds so romantic!'

'Just remember to leave off your stays and corset, men have little patience with such impediments and can fumble about with them forever.'

I found Noel Fibbit sprawled out in a chaise in the morning room. He looked up at me over a copy of *Punch*, a dour expression clouding his face.

Taking his hand in mine, I sat on the edge of the chaise. 'Four o'clock,' said I.

'What happens then?'

'Paradise.'

'I'm sorry, I don't –'

'You are to be at her door. Knock quietly.'

'You mean, Miss MacDill – Deborah?' He sat up, his features lit with a sudden glow.

'Your virgin awaits you.'

'Oh, Jenny! Thank you!'

'You must be gentle with her – very gentle, Noel.'

'Oh, I will be, indeed.' Excited, he stood, consulted his pocket watch. 'You're a marvel! How will I ever repay you?'

'I'm sure I'll think of a way.'

'My first virgin! Father will be proud of me!'

'It will be up to you to undress her . . . teach her.'

'Good Lord, it's only two thirty-five – an hour and a half to wait!'

'And you must not rush things,' said I. 'Remember, she has never known a man before.'

'Yes, yes, of course. Oh happy day! Father will be proud of me!'

Actually, thought I, none of it really mattered. We could probably have made do without the alum and blood: young Noel would probably have never noticed the difference.

Yet another venture between the walls awaited me. It was a quest that if successful, might see me leaving Fanshawe House immediately thereafter. If I found what I was looking for, it would then be a simple matter to saddle a horse in the stable and, undetected, make my way to the village where I would await the next train to London. (Saddling horses was a skill common to every blacksmith's daughter.)

However, first things, first. It was necessary that I locate the rooms that had been occupied that morning by the Swiss Dr Hochenbusch and the American Mr Smith. At 2:45, that afternoon, I passed into the labyrinth.

Of the eleven bedrooms to which I had access, six of them (my own included) had been previously occupied. That left five. The first of these was still empty. Thirty yards farther on I came on the second, previously un-occupied room. It was obviously serving now as the bedchamber assigned to the 'new' house guest, Mademoiselle Babette Chartreuse.

Through the peephole, I was delighted to find 'Mademoiselle' in bed, entertaining my old friend Mr Stubbs. Naked, she lay on her back, her legs spread wide and aloft like two shapely flagstaffs. Mr Stubbs was poised between them, supporting himself on his arms. His muscular arse pumped furiously as he pistoned in and out of her. Beneath him, her body undulating wildly, Babette was manipulating her clitoris with one hand whilst with the other she pinched one of Mr Stubbs's nipples. Growing more randy by the second, I watched as she drew her legs back, locking them about her lover's neck. It was a delightful, arse-elevating posture that I myself valued most highly as it lent itself to the deepest possible penetration. Babette seemed of a like mind. With ever-increasing gusto, she extracted full benefit from the mutually advantageous configuration: acting and reacting with abandoned thrustings and rotations of her voluptuous bottom.

'Twas indeed a lusty tableau! As a clandestine observer, I found myself responding lasciviously, not only to the sights but also to the sounds of passion – the squeals, whimpers, pantings, moans, and groans of ecstasy, the rhythmic slappings of fervent fuckery! As if by its own volition, my hand made its way under my skirt to the naked dampness of an awakening quim. I felt an all-encompassing sympathy with the ecstatic female who before my very eyes was undergoing such a tempestuous fucking. They were my legs about his neck! My arse cheeks being slapped with insistent rhythm! My cunt swallowing his distended organ to the very hilt!

But then, suddenly, I found myself brought up short with the realization that this was not the time for lewd caprice. For moments a prurient desire made war on my will. But enough! I steeled myself against the lewd temptation. Britain must come first! Duty awaited and I must get on with it.

With some reluctance, I made my way a few yards along the passageway, then down a ladder, and onward for a few yards until finally I arrived at another room that had been empty the day before. Now, however, I could see that it was occupied. A large steamer trunk took up most of the far corner and there were items of masculine apparel scattered about.

I entered through a hidden portal built into the back wall of an armoire. Draped across a chair was a maroon velvet smoking jacket. The label inside read: JOHN WANAMAKER AND COMPANY, PHILADELPHIA. No doubt I was standing in the bedchamber of the American, Mr Samuel Smith.

I began by searching the steamer trunk and was shocked to find a pistol hidden under a stack of underdrawers. Though the ugly thing was not the object of my quest, I experienced a strong yet inexplicable desire to steal it.

I searched every conceivable hiding place: beneath chairs, mattress, bed, and carpet, between the pages of books, in the folds of the London *Times* . . . everywhere, it was all to no avail. As I was about to admit defeat, my eyes lit upon a leather portfolio on one of the bedside tables. Of course, thought I! He had no knowledge of potential thieves. Why would he attempt to hide it?

Impatiently, I unbuckled the strap, releasing the latch. Inside were stacked a thick sheaf of papers. Each was an ornate document, obviously printed from hand-engraved plates. *100 Shares – Suez Canal Company.*

Eureka! They had been in full view whilst I searched obscure hiding places! Now all that remained was to find the shares brought from Switzerland by Dr Hochenbusch.

I removed the certificates from the portfolio. Then, taking the London *Times*, I proceeded quickly to tear and fold in order to create a similar bulk. This I inserted carefully into the briefcase. I snapped the latch shut, then buckled the strap and replaced the thing on the table where I'd found it.

About to leave, I recalled the pisol in the steamer trunk. Dumbly, I knew not why, I proceeded hurriedly to the trunk where I wrapped the horrid thing in a pair of Mr Smith's drawers. Then, burdened with stock certificates and pistol, I exited Mr Smith's bedchamber through the same cunning trapdoor I had used to enter.

Once more I was between the walls. I found the very next room to be occupied by Dr Hochenbusch. Peering through the peephole, I observed the large man involved in a strange activity. He lay naked, faceup on the floor. Alternately he bent forward to touch his toes then fell back till once again he rested on the floor. The ritual was repeated over and over again in rhythmic cadence. Try as I could, I could divine no logical purpose behind the strenuous and unusual enterprise. Could it be, I conjectured, an exotic form of masturbation? It took but a moment for me to realize that such was not the case, as his handsome, though flaccid penis, flopped about, obviously uninterested in the weird exertions of its master.

Though I couldn't hear him distinctly, Dr Hochenbusch seemed to count aloud each time his outstretched fingers made contact with his toes. As I watched, with growing impatience, he remained at the meaningless game for some two or three additional minutes. Then without pause, he rolled over. Supporting his body on hands and toes, he proceeded to lower himself until his chin made contact with the floor. Next, he straightened his arms and raised his body to its previous position in order to repeat the process. Up and down he went, touching only his chin to the floor each time. Again he was counting. Though his penis remained soft, his muscles did not. Arms, belly, shoulders, and legs bulged magnificently. Could it be, I reasoned, that his unusual activity was designed to reduce the size of these oversized (and perhaps grotesque?) muscles by working them to death.

Finally, Dr Hochenbusch ceased the game and stood. As he dressed I surveyed the room through my peephole with a thorough eye. There atop a large chest were the shares! My mission would soon be concluded! I would wait him out. When he left the room, his shares too would be mine. The Suez Canal would remain safe for the empire! Before anyone at Fanshawe House realized they were missing, I would be in London, handing the certificates to the Prince of Wales!

Fickle fate decided otherwise. I watched with increasing trepidation as Dr Hochenbusch, fully clothed now, rolled and tied the certificates with a blue silk ribbon. Then, abruptly, certificates in hand, he was out the door. It all happened quickly before my very eyes. For moments, in a state of confusion, I stared fixedly into the empty bedchamber. Breathing deeply, I calmed myself in an effort to think clearly. *I possessed half the shares. Would there be a second oportunity to lay my hands on the other half?* It struck me that the doctor was probably, even now, on his way to hand them over to Sir Harry. *If Mr Smith were to do likewise with his certificates, the game would be up! Surely someone – Sir Harry, most likely – would open the portfolio to check its contents. The London* Times *would be my undoing!*

I must hasten back to Mr Smith's room to replace his certificates! After that I could await a more opportune time to repossess them along with the doctor's. All or nothing!

I raced through the labyrinth. With pounding heart I placed my eye to Mr Smith's peephole. Fear gripped as if I'd been suddenly drenched in ice water! The portfolio was gone!

With my single candle growing shorter, I hurried to the Fibbit bedchamber to find it unoccupied. Then, breathing heavily, I made my way rapidly to the peephole over-looking the ground-floor study.

The three men were there. Mr Smith and Dr Hochenbusch were seated in high-backed leather wing chairs. As I watched, Sir Harry lit their cigars, then seating himself behind the desk, he proceeded to light his own.

My heart skipped a beat. There atop the very desk at which, daily, I worked on Sir Harry's memoirs, were Dr Hochenbusch's stock certificates! The beribboned roll lay next to Mr Samuel Smith's portfolio . . . *but the slim and elegant leather case contained naught but a back number of the London Times! I possessed the shares. Even now I clutched them nervously in my right hand, attempting frantically to will them back to whence they came!*

'Gentlemen,' said Sir Harry Fibbit, 'your part in this most difficult business is concluded. All that remains is to arrange your payment for a job well done.'

'How do you propose doing that?' said the handsome Sam Smith, exhaling a lungful of blue smoke.

'My banker, Mr Stubbs, will arrange the transfer of funds, in whatever currency you desire, to the bank of your choice. I must add that he knows nothing of our little game or of the Suez shares. It must remain that way.' Sir Harry laid a hand on the roll of stock certificates. 'Mr Stubbs's function is that of a legitimate banker, nothing more.'

'Then may I take it,' said Dr Hochenbusch, 'that he is a patriotic and loyal Englishman?'

'Yes,' said Sir Harry sourly. 'As am I. I bear wounds from Afghanistan to prove it. What wounds do you bear, doctor?'

'None, Sir Harry. There is no such thing as a patriotic Swiss.'

Sir Harry turned to Mr Smith. 'And you, Sam?'

'Little Round Top at Gettysburg. I bear Yankee scar on my right arse cheek.'

'Face-to-face with the enemy.' Sir Harry Fibbit chuckled and began to untie the ribbon. 'Mine is on the left buttock. We are birds of a feather.'

'Doves, no doubt,' said a grinning Samuel Smith. 'Now about the payment . . .' He drew deeply on his cigar. 'I'm not interested in bank drafts or transfers or anything of that nature. Cash is my middle name.'

'Whatever you desire, Sam.'

'Pounds sterling. I like your little country. Think I'll stay here awhile.'

'Then allow me to welcome you to our sacred isle.'

I watched as Sir Harry, cigar clenched between his teeth, unwound the blue ribbon, laid the shares flat, and began counting. Surely Mr Smith's portfolio would be next. Would he suspect me? But there was no reason to . . . unless . . . his son Noel Fibbit were forced to tell him of the secret passageways and my knowledge of them!

Sir Harry, seemingly satisfied with the count, rerolled the shares and tied the ribbon. 'It's all there,' he said. 'Well done, doctor.'

Dr Hochenbusch nodded. Then, as I watched through a thick blue haze of cigar smoke Sir Harry sprang the latch on the portfolio. As he unbuckled the straps I realized that I had no alternative but to get to London quickly with what I had. Would it be enough? I stopped breathing as he raised the flap. 'Twas the moment of truth . . .

There was a knock on the door. Sir Harry closed the flap as Mr Stubbs entered.

'Ah, good. Right on time,' said Sir Harry. 'Now we can get on with it.' He snapped shut the latch as I began breathing again.

It was, I realized, obvious that Sir Harry did not want his banker, Mr Stubbs, to know the contents of the portfolio. Perhaps I was being presented with a second chance.

'Help yourself to a cigar.'

Mr Stubbs picked one from the desktop humidor. He rolled it in his fingers, clipped the end, then seated himself in one of the small chairs. 'Now what can I do for you gentlemen,' he said.

'Just a small transaction,' said Sir Harry, doing up the leather straps. 'Merely the simple matter of a bank transfer and some cash from the special account.'

Mr Stubbs lit up, adding an additional puff of smoke to

the general miasma. He drew a small notebook from his breast pocket.

'Five thousand pounds for each of these gentlemen,' said Sir Harry, rising from behind the desk.

'Account number two-oh-seven,' said Dr Hochenbusch. 'Heineman Bank, Zurich.'

As Mr Stubbs jotted the information I watched Sir Harry crossing the room, in his hand the portfolio, under his arm the beribboned roll of certificates. Grasping the bottom of a small oil portrait on the near wall, he pushed it upward to reveal a small wall safe. I observed carefully, my attention diverted from the conversation of the others, as he spun the dial. Left . . . sixteen; right . . . four; left . . . ten . . .

Sir Harry turned to add something to the discussion. When he turned back, his body stood between me and the safe. In a moment it was opened. I had missed the fourth number!

No matter, thought I. It would take time, but since I had the first three numbers, trial and error would surely reveal the fourth. Mr Stubbs was saying, '. . . then, if you will be good enough to come to Barclay's on Tuesday at about eleven, Mr Smith, I will have the banknotes for you.'

'You can call me Sam.'

'Well, in that case we can also have a spot of lunch,' said Mr Stubbs.

'Now,' said Sir Harry expansively, 'that we're finished with business, what say all of you to some time in the gym?'

'Excellent suggestion,' said Dr Hochenbusch.

I watched as they left the room. With my eye still to the hole, I considered entering it to deal with the safe. But it took only a moment for me to realize that such a step would be foolhardy. At this hour of the day almost anyone was liable to come into the room. It was much safer to do it late at night when there was little chance of being interrupted. I turned away from the peephole into blackness.

My candle had consumed itself and was gone. Leaning back against the wall, I digested what I had just observed and at the same time attempted to deal with the new problem. It would be dangerous to try to return all the way to my own room through the dark corridors. I must emerge from the passageway somewhere else. But what if I were seen carrying the certificates?

A few yards down the passageway was an entrance into the morning room. Using the wall to guide me, I reached its peephole. The room was deserted. Exploring carefully, I found the latch handle. A few seconds later I emerged through a sliding panel in the wainscoting.

I folded the certificates into a copy of the *Manchester Guardian* I found on the table. Then with innocent demeanour and casual step I left the morning room to make my way upstairs.

TEN

A woman's buttocks, more than any other part of her body, transmits the results of love's labours. In the heat of passion, these delightful pneumatic orbs tremble, twitch, undulate, shake, squirm, flex, pulsate, quiver, wriggle, and jerk. Each individual, voluptuous movement, as perceived by the sensitive palms of a knowledgeable lover, signifies a specific degree or state of rapture. It is a language of love that should be studied by all those men who aspire to be great lovers. [Edgar Allan Poe]

'Please, call me Rose,' said Mrs Carnaby. 'And I will call you Jenny—'tis such a lovely name.'

I had passed her room on the way to mine: Mrs Carnaby had seen me and invited me in for a glass of Madeira. We shared a small couch near the window, engaging in chitchat. She was gracious and quite friendly.

'Have you any idea what a "Jim" is?' said I, placing the copy of the *Manchester Guardian* on her dressing table.

'I think not. 'Tis a strange word. Where'd you run across it?'

'I overhead Sir Harry use it. It seems to be a place to which one would go.'

'For what purpose, my dear?'

'I haven't the remotest idea,' said I.

After a thorough discussion of the weather, she laid a hand on my knee, and speaking in a quiet, sincere voice, she said, 'I must thank you for coming to my niece's aid.'

Taken aback, I smiled weakly and nodded. How could she know of my secret dealings with Deborah? Was she, I wondered nervously, engaging in a nasty facetiousness that was merely the prelude to an angry outburst?

'I should never have thought of it myself?' she said. 'Alum! How cunning. And the vial of blood is utter genius!'

There was no mistaking her sincerity, her good nature, I was immediately at my ease. 'Mrs Carnaby,' said I, 'you are—'

'Rose, my dear,' said she.

'Ah yes . . .Rose,' said I. 'I was about to say that you are a most uncommon chaperon.'

'It would seem,' said she, with a little laugh, 'that I'm the best kind . . .at least from the point of view of she who is being chaperoned.'

'Indeed,' said I, echoing her laugh.

Mrs Carnaby refilled our glasses. 'Ten years ago, my sister Carrie and her husband — Deborah's parents — were killed when the *Anglo-Saxon* went down in a storm off Cape Race. So, you see, I am somewhat more than an aunt and a chaperon; since my husband's death last year, I have been Deborah's sole guardian.'

'And a superlative one, I'm sure.'

'I pray that is true, but since I've had no offspring of my own, my experience in rearing young ladies is, of course, limited. Nevertheless, one does the best one can. For example, just a few months ago I realized that my niece was fast approaching the age at which virginity becomes a burden. Since I believe strongly in proper education, particularly for young ladies, I rose to my responsibility. After sampling a number of men — knowledgeable and dedicated teachers are indeed a rarity — I chose the oldest of the candidates. He was a talented poet of great sensitivity, and above all a true gentleman who loved, understood, and respected women. It required a great deal of convincing on my part as he was most highly principled. But fifty quid turned the trick.'

'A superlative choice. Young maidens are rarely so fortunate.'

'Thank you, my dear. 'Twould have been a bargain at three times the price. He was a wondrous teacher. But then Deborah, being quite naive, made the unfortunate error of leading young Noel Fibbit to believe she was still a virgin. I had neglected to tell her that virginity, except under rare circumstances, is a state that knowledgeable ladies never lie about.' Her fingers tightened on my leg. 'But thanks to you, at this moment, in my niece's bed, that problem is being resolved.' She brought her face to within inches of mine, our eyes locked. 'I could kiss you in appreciation.'

'Please do . . .'

It was a friendly kiss, quite sisterly. When our lips parted, I found her looking questioningly into my eyes. I closed mine and waited. This time her tongue probed gently, searching for a response. I spread my lips slighty, demurely, allowing it to gain entrance.

In moments, I was engaged in an exquisite lingual duel. Delicate fingers caressed the back of my neck, explored the sensitive flesh of my earlobes, the smooth skin of my throat. With an expectant shiver of full surrender, I threw my head back as her soft lips and fluttering tongue followed the same sensuous route.

Finally, she stood, grasping my wrists to raise me to my feet. With her hands on my hips, she stood before me at arm's length. I was aware of a delicious warmth suffusing my groin. I glanced quickly at the dressing table. The newspaper lay there where I had left it, the certificates hidden safely in its fold. All was right with the world.

'Please,' she said, 'I must see you naked.'

'Yes.' With no hesitation, I reached behind me to undo the uppermost clasp of my dress.

'And you shall see me.'

'Ah yes, that would be delightful.'

Separated by but a few feet, we disrobed. In minutes, our clothing was heaped at our feet. We stood, facing one another, totally nude.

With wide eyes and parted lips, Mrs Carnaby surveyed me from head to toe. For moments she seemed speechless.

'How lovely you are,' said I.

'And you, dear Jenny,' said she, finding her voice, 'are the most beautiful woman I have ever laid eyes on.'

'And you are delicious . . .'

'Ah, then you will enjoy tasting me . . .'

'Your breasts are so plump,' said I. 'like ripe melons.'

'I was told of your beauty,' said she, 'but could hardly believe such superlatives. Now I see that they barely do you justice.'

'Who spoke of me?'

'Sir Harry, Lady Doris, Mr Aziz, my niece, and the young man, who, thanks to you, is even now enjoying her favours. Each of them outdid the others in praise of your vivacity, your lascivious talents, your passionate devotion to shared pleasures, and above all, your beauty. Now, I will join the chorus.'

My naked body flushed in embarrassment at the excessive nature of her compliment. But nevertheless it was a distinct pleasure hearing such praise.

We were in each other's arms, pressing lips and bodies together. Rose inserted a leg between mine. I pressed down against it, riding it slowly back and forth.

'We fit so well,' she said, 'and yet our bodies are so different. Yours is like a gazelle.'

'Your hips are so full and wide and comforting,' said I, insinuating playful fingers into the cleft between her plump buttocks.

In a trice we were on the bed. She hovered above me, pinching my nipple between gentle fingers whilst the fingers of her other hand cavorted featherlike down the length of my body. I twisted about till my head lay just under her breast. She cupped it gracefully, feeding it to my eager mouth. I sucked, then pulled away to circumnavigate a pink aureole with fluttering tongue. She groaned in appreciation as we rolled over onto our sides. Her free hand reached between my legs to cup one of my buttocks. A delightfully intrusive wrist pressed against my quim. I rotated my bottom in slow, sensuous circles.

'Ah, Jenny,' she said, squeezing my undulating arse-cheek. 'Your puss is awakening. I can feel the juices rising.'

'And yours?' I reached down between her thighs. My questing finger danced about in outer folds sodden with female dew. 'Lovely,' said I. 'You're gushing.'

'Ah Jenny, aren't we lewd?'

Humping against her wrist, I moaned a reply, ran a gentle finger down the length of her clitoris. She trembled and pulled me up to her. We kissed, long and passionately, rubbing our bodies together.

She spoke in low, almost whispering tones. 'Shall we do what French ladies do?'

'*Soixante-neuf*?'

'Yes . . .'twould be lovely.'

A truly magical number.'

'The most ingenious and voluptuous in all of numerology.'

We assumed the position, myself on the bottom. Then with my lips just inches away from its succulent target, I inhaled deeply, savouring the piquant fragrance. It left my head spinning – an uncanny bouquet of sweet perfume blended with the natural, spicy aroma of female prurience. Emitting a little squeal of delight, I grasped her buttocks, pulled her down, and buried my face in the deliciously aromatic nest of love. Drawing her labia into my mouth I sucked on it as if it were treacle toffee.

At the same time her mouth was committed to a similar joyful tour. Her tongue ran the length of my garden, lapping back and forth until finally its tip insinuated itself into the twitching orifice. With a passionate little squeal she reached up to grasp each of my buttocks and pull my undulated nether parts down into even tighter contact with her face.

'Suck,' she muttered into my pussy. 'Suck it, Jenny.'

102

Mrs Carnaby's quim unfolded like the petals of an exotic flower, opening itself to my worshipful tongue. I drank from her — thrilling to the ambrosial taste, my moans of pleasure muffled by cunt flesh. Then, reaching beneath her, I grasped her pneumatic bum cheeks even tighter, as they transmitted her passion via muscular contractions.

My face was lost in Rose's cunt. I felt for her clitoris, tested the less sensitive upper part, ran my tongue up and down the sides, teasing it into even fuller erection, building slowly — ever so slowly — toward what I knew would be a shattering climax.

Rose was doing likewise, paying lascivious court to my clit. I quivered to a wildfire of sensations. Passionately, I took her clitoris between my lips, tweaked its fat, unsheated base with my tongue tip. Faster and faster! Our tempos matched — rhythms and couterrhythms — a symphonic battery of lust! As did mine, her throbbings grew into twitches, the twitches into tremors, the tremors into convulsions.

'Ahhh, feel me cummmm!' she cried, raising her head from my open crotch, then diving again into its pulsating wetness. 'Now, Jennnyyy!' My tongue lashed her clitoris.

We climaxed in tandem, both of us moaning our joy into the heat of seething cunts.

A century later she raised her dripping face from between my thighs to smile at me. We sat up, kissing each other tenderly — tasting ourselves.

'Lovely,' she said, running her tongue across her lips.

'Lovely, indeed,' said I.

I made sure to take my copy of the *Manchester Guardian* with me when I left. Then, once back in my own room. I used a fireplace poker to pry up a floorboard in the secret corridor. There, just a few feet to the right of the hidden access, I secreted both pistol and stock certificates.

It had already been a long day. I had no doubt, however, that for me, it had barely begun.

ELEVEN

All of us, no matter what our persuasions, crave applause.
Those who say otherwise are surely either liars, hypocrites,
or self-hating wretches. [Elleander Morning]

'A toast,' said Sir Harry, 'to our beautiful Miss Deborah
MacDill, who has just recently given up her maidenhood
to enter into the realm of true womanhood!'

We all raised our glasses to Deborah, who blushed
becomingly. Her Aunty Rose, seated two places down,
smiled at me, tilting her glass furtively in my direction.
'Twas a surreptitious tribute that brought a similar blush
to my own cheeks.

Sir Harry led the way with: 'For she's a jolly good
fellow . . .' we all joined in.

'Speech!'

We were silent as Deborah raised her glass in turn. She
spoke quietly, with a brief but significant glance at me in
mid sentence. 'I owe it all to a most talented, sensitive, and
inventive lover who managed, with verve, intelligence, and
tenacity, to overcome all barriers.'

'Bravo!'

'From this day on,' said Mr Aziz in a high-pitched voice,
'may you labour long and pleasurably in the garden of
lust!'

'Here, here!'

'And a toast,' said Samuel Smith, 'to the lucky rascal
who changed you for the better.'

104

'But who is he?' said Mademoiselle Babette. All eyes turned to Deborah. She glanced across the table at Noel, then smiling shyly, said in a small voice. 'It was Master Noel Fibbit who deflowered me so exquisitely at tea time this very afternoon.'

'Here, here!'

'As a proud father, I propose a toast to an intrepid son.'

'Hip-hip, hooray!'

'Speech.'

The young Fibbitt stood. In a voice tinged with shyness, he said, 'I take pride in my accomplishment and thank you all for your recognition. I must say, however, that it would have all come to naught without the acquiescence and cooperation of my lovely partner, Miss MacDill . . . couldn't have done it alone, you see. But there is one other here – she knows who she is – who contributed greatly to our successful mating. I feel I must extend my gratitude –'

'And who was that?'

'Yes, tell us.'

'Just how, old chap, did she contribute?'

'She counselled me. She arranged time and place.'

'And much more,' said Deborah MacDill.

'Pray, tell us who.'

'I'm afraid 'twould be unseemly to disclose her name.'

'Spoken like a true gentleman!'

'Here, here!'

'A toast to the unknown lady.'

'To the silent partner, whomever she may be.'

'Here, here!'

'And to a long life of grand debauchery for all!'

'Here, here!'

Pleasantries, chitchat, and a delightful selection of French wines accompanied the soup, the fish, and a most delicious pheasant under glass that was served with truffles and the inevitably dull carrots and brussel sprouts usually to be found on one's plate at every Fanshawe House meal.

Over fruit and cheese – a beautifully aged Stilton – Sir Harry tapped his glass to hush the tittle-tattle. 'In the light of this recent event,' he said, 'would it not be appropriate – truly fascinating – for some of the ladies present to describe their initial experience with Cupid's tumescent dart?'

'It would be most educational,' said Mr Aziz.

'And what of the gentlemen?' said Rose Carnaby. 'Surely they should be included?'

'Gentlemen's tales are not nearly so interesting.' said Mr Stubbs.

'Quite true,' said Dr Hochenbusch. 'I've no doubt that my own experience would seem a bore.'

'A bore or an embarrassment?' muttered Rose Carnaby, under her breath.

'Men are never actually virgins,' said Mr Aziz.

'Here, here!'

'May I speak for the ladies?' said I.

'Yes do – be our spokeswoman – by all means,' said the ladies.

'Gentlemen,' said I. 'Each of us at this table, female *and* male, was once a virgin. Therefore, each has a story to tell. As women we are all fascinated by the viewpoint of the dominant sex, which is so different from our own. I speak for the ladies when I say that if we are to play Sir Harry's charming game, some of the men should also be included.'

'Ladies first,' said Sam Smith.

'But I must insist on absolute truth,' said Sir Harry.

'Here, here,' cried the ladies.

'Then,' said Sir Harry, 'let us hear first from Mrs Carnaby.'

Rose Carnaby lowered her wineglass, glanced about the table, then with a rueful smile began. 'My mother, like myself, was widowed while still young. Those of you who are beyond a "certain" age will recall the Opium War. My father was shot dead whilst marching into Canton with the Coldstream Guards.'

'God save the Queen.'

106

'After a suitable period of mourning my mother took her first lover. We were making the Grand Tour at the time — 'twas socially permissible for unescorted widows to do so, even then. I was eighteen years old and quite pretty.'

'Ah, then it is easy to see, madam, that you have grown, over the years, from a pretty girl into a beautiful woman.'

'Here, here!'

'Thank you, to be sure.' said Rose Carnaby with a gracious smile. 'The term *beautiful* would most certainly have applied to my mother. We were in Venice at the time and there were quite a few gallants of varied ages and social status sniffing about — as Italians are wont to do. My mother chose not the handsomest of these, as one might expect, but rather, the least handsome. Giuseppe was unlike most of these roving, Latin lovers. He was neither count, gigolo, nor wealthy scion. His figure was far from perfect, his clothes far from superbly cut. In short he was an artist — a composer.'

Rose Carnaby paused for a moment to sip from her glass. 'It was spring in Venice, certainly the best of time and place. Ah, that afternoon my mother spent secluded with her Italian lover . . . I remember it clearly, as if it were yesterday. Whilst she bedded him, I spent a glorious day floating about happily in a gondola, seeing the sites while being serenaded by a most handsome and romantic gondolier.

'That evening the three of us took dinner together. I was impressed by Giuseppe; he was a deeply sensitive and at the same time a charmingly witty man who spoke about as much English as my mother and I spoke Italian. We all understood one another and he flirted with both of us outrageously.

'At breakfast the next morning my mother began the day quite strangely. It was as if she had something to say but could not manage to phrase it properly. Finally at lunch, she blurted it out. "Rose," said she, "you are eighteen, and somewhat mature for your age. Perhaps it is time you became a woman."

'I said, "You mean marriage, mama?"

'"I'm sure that will happen eventually," said she, "when

we return to England and you meet a suitable young man. But that's not what I speak of."

'"Then," said I, "What *are* you speaking of?"

'"It is time," said she, almost in a whisper, "that you gave yourself to a man. Are you shocked?"

'"Yes, Mama," said I, my cheeks growing flushed, even as a strange warmth coursed through my body.

'"Oh heavens," said she. "This is liable to be difficult."

'"But I agree, Mama . . . I think . . . it is time . . ."

'"Thank heaven," said she. "You see, I am concerned for your health. After eighteen years or at most twenty, there is a tendency for sensitive, developed young maidens to become morose. Virginity develops into a chronic disease. I know this to be a fact as I myself suffered it."

'"But shouldn't one be in love?" said I.

'"Yes," said she, "but not with every man. That would be a terrible strain."

'"Then who?" said I.

'"Giuseppe," said she. "He is gentle and understanding and a marvellous lover. He says he would be honoured by the privilege to make a woman of you. You will learn much from him."'

Rose glanced at me, a twinkle lighting her eyes, I thought. As went the mother, so goes the aunt. 'It wasn't till later,' continued Rose, 'when I realized that in addition to choosing Giuseppe from amongst all the potential lovers in Venice, my mother had actually tested him in bed to make sure he would be right for me.'

'A shining example,' said Mr Stubbs, 'of the most noble of all attributes: mother love.'

'Here, here!'

'Indeed, it is,' said Rose Carnaby. 'And mother chose well. The very next night, she went to the opera with a friend, leaving me to be tutored by Giuseppe. Ah, how lovely! And as it transpired. I spent an entire week with him . . . dear man. It was a love affair I will always remember. I am sure he felt likewise. About three months after Mother and I returned to England, I received a love letter from him stating that I was the inspiration for an opera he was composing. It was to be called *Rigoletto*.'

'Good heavens,' said Lady Doris. ' 'Twas Giuseppe Verdi himself who deflowered you!'

'Not exactly, Lady Doris,' said Mrs Carnaby. 'The actual ceremony was conducted the day before by my romantic gondolier as we floated about near the Lido. Signor Verdi, being a man of the world, was not surprised when he discovered my lack of a maidenhead and was gentleman enough not to inform my mother. The knowledge that her daughter had not been a virgin would have saddened her deeply.'

'A lovely story,' said Deborah MacDill.

'One can say that you managed to eat you cake and have it,' said Sir Harry.

'Here, here!'

Next to be called upon was the American, Mr Sam Smith. He leaned back in his chair, smiled ruefully, and said. 'I was a soldier, just turned nineteen, which in England, I guess would be considered an advanced age for a virgin. I was in the cavalry under General Crook – George Crook – the great Indian fighter. The young lady was a Shoshone girl, cute as a button, and I'd guess, four or five years younger than I. We had just defeated her tribe after chasing them halfway across the Nevada Territory. The Shoshone fought bravely but, lacking the leadership, showed none of the brilliant tactics of the Sioux or the Comanche. We routed them with ease. Now they live on a reservation in California.

'The girl's name was Kachese. Sounds like a sneeze. It's a simple story, really. It happened the second night after the battle. It was late, most of the campfires had burned down. I was hunkered deep in my bedroll under a skyful of stars and a waning moon. 'Twas then I saw her. She was silhouetted on a low ridge barely twenty or thirty yards away. No mistaking that it was an Indian woman. Even in silhouette it was easy to see she wasn't white. White ladies, sad to say, don't go about half naked. I lay there, watching her, wondering how she had gotten past the pickets. She stood with her legs apart, her hands by her sides – a lovely sight even in the dark. But one can never tell with Indians. She might be the bait for some kind of newfangled Indian ambushing trick. I got up and quietly strapped my pistol belt on over my longjohn underwear. She had to have seen me, but she didn't move. I loosened the snap on the holster and made towards her.

'I thought for sure she'd run from me, but she didn't. She just stood, poised like a pretty little statue, till I was about ten feet from her. As I got closer, I could see she was even more beautiful . . . but wait now, there's something I have to say, before I go on . . .' Sam Smith leaned forward, his arms on the table. As he spoke, his eyes darted about, settling on each of us in turn. 'The idea of a *beautiful* Indian woman would have been inconceivable to many of my peers, a contradiction in terms. White folks in my country don't think much of Indians. In fact they think less of them than they do of niggers. I mean lately they've conceded that niggers are human; that hasn't happened yet with Indians. I don't hold with such views and that's one of the reasons why I'm going to settle right here in England.'

'But you fought for the South in your recent Civil War, old boy,' said Sir Harry.

'That was just out of cussedness. If we'd have won, I would have become the first abolitionist in the Confederate State of America.'

'Welcome to Britain,' said Rose Carnaby. 'But you should know that we too have our Indians – East Indians – and think of them much the same way as you do your countrymen.'

'I beg your pardon, madam,' said Mr Stubbs. 'We don't think of *our* Indians as being nonhuman.'

'Then how do you explain – '

'Inferior, perhaps,' continued Mr Stubbs, 'in the ways of civilization, but human beings nonetheless.'

'Inferior,' said Mrs Carnaby, 'is your word, not mine. Despite their faults, 'twas Americans who stated that "all men are created equal."'

'I too hold to that,' said Mr Stubbs. 'And 'tis the white man's burden to bring that concept to fruition!'

'Ladies – Gentleman,' said Sir Harry. 'Perhaps we might let Mr Smith get on with it.'

'Sorry.'

'Where was I?' said Mr Smith.

'The Indian maiden on the ridge.'

'Ah, yes. As I approached her she sank to the ground. I stood, hovering over her. Even as I watched she removed the halter that covered her breasts, and then the leather loincloth that covered the rest of her. She was naked! 'Twas the first nude female I had ever seen in the flesh! She placed a finger to her chest, whispering, "Kachese." I did likewise, croaking, "Sam."

'I was rooted to the spot. Unlike so many in my regiment, I had never held with rape, which helps explain why I was still a virgin. Raping Indian women was a game many of them played. I felt, even then, that there could be no pleasure in bedding a woman who had no desire to be bedded. That's not a moral attitude, merely an aesthetic one.'

'You do yourself an injustice, my friend,' said Mr Stubbs.

'Perhaps,' said Sam Smith. 'But, be that as it may, there before me, in the Nevada night, was an actual invitation! My first! It was the stuff of dreams. Nevertheless, I stood as if petrified. Having no education in such matters, I didn't know quite what to do next. Perhaps if I'd had time to prepare myself . . .'

'Poor boy,' said Lady Doris.

'Well, that Indian girl knew what to do and that's for sure! She just reached up and grabbed hold. When she let go, a couple seconds later, my prick was making a big bulge in my drawers. I was out of them in a trice, pausing only to remove my damned-fangled pistol belt.

'She rolled over, assuming an ass-high stance on her hands and knees. I didn't know quite where to put it, but once more she saved the day by reaching between her legs and grabbing hold again. I was so excited, I almost spent in her hand. But within a few seconds she had guided me to the portal. Once there, my quandry was solved. Instinct took over. I thrust home! Ah, what a feeling – that first entry! I just let it soak, deep inside, then as she groaned her approval I began to stroke. I came on the fourth, paused, and then started again, fucking in my own warm spunk.

'The second fuck took little longer; all of three minutes, I recall. The third and fourth effort took perhaps ten or fifteen minutes. Must have shot a full pint of spunk, all told – leastwise that's how it felt.'

'Ah, to be young again,' said Mr Aziz.

'How true.' Sam Smith laughed. 'Well, the next thing I knew, I was on my back catching my breath and the pretty little Indian girl, with my jism dripping down the inside of her thighs, was standing over me with my very own Colt in her hand! It was pointed right between my eyes! Damn! I'd really been taken for a fool! Before I could react she jerked the trigger. Thank God she jerked it, rather than squeezed it. It threw her aim off and saved my life. The slug hit my shoulder with the force of an express train!

'In a state of confusion, I watched as she threw down my pistol, retrieved her "clothing," and made off to the east. Thinking quickly, before the pain set in, I picked up the revolver and fired a shot in the air. All hell had broken loose in the camp; lamps were being lit all over the place. Someone was shouting orders. 'Twas a devil of a fuss! I stood up, fired one more shot in the air. "Over here!" I shouted. "Three mounted Indians . . . they took off toward the west!" Then I fainted from the pain.

'When I came to in the surgeon's tent, about half an hour

later, I found out that some of our fellows had taken off in hot pursuit of the enemy. A damned fool thing to do in the dark. But of course there was no enemy, except for Kachese, and she had gone the other way.'

'But she shot you in cold blood!' said Dr Hockenbusch.

'Well,' said Sam Smith, grinning widely. 'I don't think her blood was all that cold. I remember her as a hot-blooded little wench. She was probably avenging the death of a brother or father; using all her faculties to make war on the enemy, who unfortunately happened to be me.'

'But what she did was hardly cricket, old boy,' said Mr Stubbs.

'Only you British think of war as cricket. It is not, by God! One uses the weapons that come to hand, which is exactly what we did. It was no more immoral than any other kind of ambush. She was a brave warrior – unarmed – so in order to shoot me, she had to get at my pistol.' He laughed 'She sucked me into attacking from the rear and then surrounded me . . . tactics worthy of old General Crook himself!'

'And you let her get away! Why?'

'If they caught her, they would have killed her. But I had no such grudge. What I mean to say is that making love to that little squaw might not have been worth dying for, but it was certainly worth a wounded shoulder. Hell, if it hadn't been for her, I might still be a virgin.'

'I wish,' said Lady Doris, 'that it was in our power to award you some sort of medal for gallantry. You deserve it.'

'Here, here!'

'And one for the Indian maid,' said I.

'Here, here!'

'And did you really spend four times in just a few minutes?'

'It must have taken about twenty, near as I can recollect.'

'Ah, to be young again! I love it when a man fucks me

in his own spunk,' said Rose Carnaby. 'It's so deliciously lewd.'

'True, dear lady,' said Mr Aziz. 'But it is a privilege restricted to very young men as was Mr Smith at the time. These days it takes almost an hour for me to recover and start again and by that time the first cumming has turned cold.'

Sir Harry nodded. 'But the way around that problem is to fuck into the spunk of another man.'

'Even more delicious!' said Rose.

'Indeed.'

'Or better yet, more than just one man,' said Sir Harry.

'Heavens!' said Deborah MacDill. 'Have you done that often?'

'Quite often, as I'm sure we all have. But there is one occasion that stands out.'

'Tell me, please!'

'I think it best if you hear it from my wife,' said Sir Harry. 'She, after all, was the recipient – or should I say the receptacle.'

'Receptacle, indeed,' said Lady Doris, smiling broadly.

' 'Twas a marvellous night, as I recall – about ten or twelve years ago. We were in Paris. Sir Harry provided me with eighteen young men. God only knows how he procured them. They filled our bedchamber! Eighteen beautiful young men, wielding stiff pricks! In the course of the night I was fucked at least twice by each of them while Sir Harry drank champagne and watched.'

'Good Lord!'

'You did nothing but watch?' said Sam Smith.

'Well, I didn't masturbate, if that's what you mean,' said Sir Harry.

'How could you not?'

'I disciplined myself. You see, I wanted to conserve it.'

'But he did other things,' said Lady Doris. 'He participated quite nicely, actually. He sucked on some of the fellows to keep them hard for me. I loved watching

114

that, just as much as he enjoyed me being fucked. Sir Harry is such a thoughtful and accommodating husband. In one instance he masturbated one of the young men almost to orgasm and then just as the fellow was about to cum, Harry guided him to join his mate deep inside me.'

'You mean you took two of those things simultaneously?' said Deborah.

'Three,' said Lady Doris. 'There was yet another implanted in my bum. 'Twas divine!'

'Oh, I get a chill just thinking about it!'

'And all three shot off at the same time,' said Lady Doris. 'It was like an artillery barrage.'

'Oh, I'd so love for that to happen to me!' said Deborah.

'I'm sure there are three amongst us who would be happy to accommodate you, my dear Miss MacDill.' said Mr Aziz.

'You can deal me in,' said Mr Smith.

'And I would be pleased,' said Dr Hochenbusch, 'to take up the rear.'

'There, you have your three gallant volunteers, Miss MacDill,' said Sir Harry.'

' 'Twould be a bit of a stretch for you, dear niece,' said Rose Carnaby. 'Lady Doris, so to speak, was somewhat more experienced.'

'How true,' said Lady Doris. 'You should entertain at least a few more pricks before attempting to swallow two at once in that tight little sheath of yours.'

'But surely, Lady Doris, you too are tight.'

'Indeed she is!' said Mr Stubbs.

'I'll vouch for that,' said Mr Smith.

'Dear girl,' said Lady Doris. ''Tis not a matter of tightness but of elasticity.'

'That will suffice for an anatomy lesson,' said Sir Harry. 'Back to the matter at hand.'

'Yes, do,' said Deborah MacDill, leaning forward.

'I had all eighteen before the night was out.'

'Good Lord, eighteen loads of spunk in your quim!' said Mr Stubbs.

'More than double that, dear man,' said Lady Doris, a note of pride in her voice. 'As I said, each of my cavaliers came at least twice. My poor battered quim runneth over, so to speak. I was filled to the brim with sweet young jism! 'Twas all stirred up and warm; thick and delicious, like Cornish clotted cream. And to add to that, a few of them came in my mouth and on my breasts, my belly . . . everywhere! I was awash with spunk!'

'Oh heavens!' said Deborah, her eyes closed.

'Sir Harry went mad with lust,' said Lady Doris. 'He licked me all over, kissed my spunky mouth – savoured it all as if I were a gourmet feast!'

'Then I fucked her in the leavings of eighteen other men!' said Sir Harry. 'My cock was immersed in perhaps thirty-five loads of jism! 'Twas lewd beyond description – one of the most most memorable nights of my life!'

'And after my sweet husband added his lovely cream to theirs, he licked my cunt . . . sucked it all out of me whilst kissing me from time to time in order to share the lovely stuff.'

'*Très formidable!*' said Mademoiselle Chartruese.

'Ah, Lady Doris,' said Mr Stubbs. 'How I envy your capacity. Women are capable of so much more than we poor men.'

'And five will get you ten that you could have managed twice what you did,' said Sam Smith.

'Thrice,' said Lady Doris.

'Many of us are as sisters to the Empress Messalina,' said I. 'Under the proper circumstances we can demonstrate an infinite capacity to take and give pleasure. Think how simple it is for a woman to pleasure six or more men simultaneously and how impossible it is for a man to do likewise.'

'Let's see,' said Sam Smith, 'you mean, one cock in each hand, one in the mouth, one in the rear and one – or perhaps two – in the cunt. Did I leave anything out?'

'Between the breasts,' said I, 'and if one is adroit, beneath each armpit.'

'And keep in mind the occasional gentleman who is addicted to silken, feminine hair,' said Rose Carnaby.

'And feet,' said Mademoiselle Chartreuse.

'Good Lord!' said Mr Stubbs. 'I count ten.'

'Eleven,' said Mr Aziz.

'And consider,' said I, 'that some women are capable of many orgasms, one following the other, ofttimes in rapid succession.'

'Ah yes,' said Mr Stubbs. 'It is not blasphemous to say that the creator made us the lesser of the breed.'

There was silence for a moment as each of us attempted to visualize the lascivious panorama so recently described. Then, Mr Aziz said, 'Perhaps, Lady Doris, should be next to speak of the loss of her virginity.'

Sam Smith laughed. 'No offence, dear lady, but from what I heard just now, I feel that perhaps you might never have been a virgin.'

Our gracious hostess, leaning back gracefully in her chair, proceeded. 'In a way, you are correct, my American friend; at the least, I wasn't aware of its actual loss. You see, at the tender age of seventeen I was a precocious horse woman . . .'

'Ah, I see,' said Dr Hochenbusch. 'The usual result of riding in an unladylike manner.'

'Indeed, my good doctor. But as I said, I was a *precocious* horsewoman. Both attributes played a part in the loss of innocence and virginity. The first of these, my precociousness, was the quality that propelled me into an unsuitable marriage. The second, my fondness of horses, particularly my fondness for riding astride rather than sidesaddle as is prescribed for respectable ladies, played, as Dr Hochenbusch has indicated, an even more direct role.

'I married Jeremy Gordon,' continued Lady Doris, 'a handsome and fashionable young man, son of Sir Malcolm Gordon, Third Duke of Westershire. The father was a staunch Tory and for a time first sea lord, until his fanatic opposition to steam power saw him out of office.

117

'Son Jeremy was no more intelligent than his father. He did, however, cut a dashing figure and it seemed as if half the women in Britain had their caps set for him. As did I.

'My strategy was to cultivate his sister, Elvira, a somewhat vacuous young lady near my own age. By making use of information so obtained I was able, time and time again, to place myself in the immediate proximity of her brother. These meetings appeared to be, almost always, accidental. He would find me (well chaperoned, of course) at the next table to his at the Savoy, in the adjacent box at Epsom races, in the adjoining stall at Covent Garden, as a fellow guest at country weekends (where I would arrange to be seated next to him at the dinner table). I chased him the length and breadth of England, flirting ourtrageously.

'Soon, as I hoped they would be, the tables were turned; I became the pursued, he the pursuer. 'Twas then I changed my tactics and made myself scarce; a method that has been practised successfully by young women since the days of the ancient Greeks. Absence, they say, makes the heart fonder.

'My campaign lasted all of nineteen weeks. At the end of this time, Jeremy Gordon asked me to marry him and I was by way of becoming the Fourth Duchess of Westershire.

'On our wedding night he pounced atop me and within seconds, with no preparation, not even a kiss, was thrusting into me unmercifully. In my ignorance, I accepted this behaviour as normal; he was, after all, a man and therefore knowledgeable about such things. As a woman, my function, thought I, was to lie back and suffer through it – you know, woman's lot and all that sort of thing. Steel yourself, close your eyes, and concentrate on Queen and country.

'A quick ejaculation ended my ordeal. But no . . . within a minute after regaining his breath, my new husband flew into a rage, accused me of being a whore!

'He had experienced no barrier to his thrustings, had

found no blood on the sheets. (Previous bouts with in-nocent servant girls had led him to expect these signs of pristine virtue.) He literally booted me out of bed and swore that never again would I be permitted there. I was relegated to a small room of my own, far removed from his.

'I did not see him for over a week. Then late one night he came to my room. Standing by my bedside, he removed his dressing gown to reveal a monstrous erection. "Touch it," he ordered.

'I reached out tentatively, laying a reluctant hand on the thing. It was sticky to the touch.

'He laughed. "It's still wet from Hilda. Ah, what a sweet succulent thing she is, with breasts and an arse like an angel." He was attempting to torment me. I pulled my hand from his prick as if from a hot stove. Hilda was an upstairs maid who, in fact, had done up my room less that two hours earlier.

'"You don't like that, do you, my sweet wife?" His voice, though pitched conversationally, resonated with an ugly undertone. It frightened me. "But why take offence? Hilda is a whore just like you—sisters under the skin."

'Then suddenly he seemed to go berserk! He ripped the nightgown from my body, pulled me from the bed. I lay on the floor at his feet, sobbing, my tears flowing as much from mortifications as from fear of this brute who was my husband.

'Grasping my hand, he pulled me erect till I was poised in a painful crouch, my head level with his groin. "And now," he said, his voice little more than a husky whisper, "you are to clean it off." He pulled my head up till his awful weapon was just inches from my face. "With your tongue, my dear."

'"No!" I was horrified!'

'But such things are delightful, no?' said Babette.

'Of course, mademoiselle,' said Lady Doris. 'As you know, nothing suits me more than indulgence in such lewd pursuits with civilized ladies and gentlemen of my choice. But at the time I was a young girl with no experience but a single rape perpetrated by a monster of a husband. I had never dreamed of such things as fellatio. And the concept that taking a man's prick in one's mouth could be *mutually* pleasurable would have been beyond my comprehension. In my mental condition at the time, I'm afraid my as-yet-underdeveloped erotic imagination could not possibly have risen to the task. Perhaps if my new husband had loved me, had been understanding, tender, I might have learned to appreciate these things with him. Even a modicum of affectionate wit would have helped matters.'

'That beast!' said Rose Carnaby.

'A horrid scoundrel.'

'The fellow should have been horsewhipped!' said Sam Smith through his teeth.

'And I would have gladly applied the whip, chérie,' said Mademoiselle Babette, her eyes glowing. 'What happened next?'

'He slapped my face. Catching me unaware, he knocked me to the floor. Once again he pulled me up by the hair. This time he held me erect as he delivered an even more stinging blow.

' "You are my wife!" he shouted. "I am lord and master and you will bloody well do as I say!"

'Dazed, I opened my eyes to stare drunkenly into a tangled forest of pubic hair. I sensed a piquant odour, something I had never smelled before. I assumed it was a masculine scent, never realizing that for the first time in my life, I was inhaling the essence of woman, the savoury aroma I was to grow to cherish as being more evocative, more sensuous than the most exotic French perfume.'

'Here, here!'

'It was, of course, the leavings of Hilda, the upstairs maid. I was shortly to become quite familiar with the scent and . . . but I get ahead of myself.

'I felt the fleshy tube of my husband's muscular cock

120

brush across my tightly clenched lips. Again he slapped me. Still I refused! There is a bloody stubborn streak in my nature that invariably reacts to the catalyst of fear. I understand that it is a male, rather than a female attribute and may therefore be viewed as a shortcoming on my part. So be it! Another slap and still another, each more brutal than the preceding. Despite the tears, my lips clenched even tighter, locking my oral portal to the insistent intruder.

'Suddenly I was being hoisted to my feet, then off them. My husband carried me to the bed, threw me down on it as if I were of no greater value than a sack of potatoes.

'Out of the corner of my eye I observed the bedroom door opening. Hilda, dressed as usual in her maid's uniform, entered my room. I attempted to sit up and wrap myself in the bedspread. My husband pushed me back down onto the bed.

'"Stay there," he said, "I'll tell you when you can move."

'Hilda stood at the side of the bed surveying my body from head to toe. She smiled as if in approval. "Good evening, Miss Doris," she said.

'Mortified, I nodded, turned away.

'"She's lovely, Mr Gordon. A most beautiful body."

'"She's a whore."

'In shame I buried my face in the pillow. I sensed he was standing beside her, both of them staring down at me. They were silent for a full minute or more.

'Finally Hilda giggled. In a high-pitched voice, she said, "Eeeh now, aren't you the randy one."

'Despite the state I was in, I felt a growing curiosity. With one eye, I peered under my arm at them. They were both standing at the edge of the bed. Hilda was naked! She was slowly frigging my husband's stiff pego with one hand whilst with the other she was frigging herself.

'"I'd just love to watch you fuck her," she said. "That would be lovely now, wouldn't it?"

'"I'll never put my prick into that filthy cunt!" His voice cracked in anger. Once again I looked away, attempting to burrow in the mattress.

'"I'm sorry sir," said Hilda. "I didn't mean . . ."

'"I'll fuck her mouth, her arse; that's all the whore is good for! But as for her cunt, I'd just as soon fuck a pig!"

'"Please, Mr Gordon," said Hilda. "She is your wife, you know."

'He was silent for a moment. "Wife, you say? Then I will treat her as such. To begin with, a good wife must acknowledge her master."

'Fear gripped me. I seemed paralysed, an innocent victim of fate. There were sounds of scurrying around, of furniture being moved. Once again I peeped. Jeremy was standing on a chair unfastening the long bell chord. Then, a moment later, he rolled me over onto my stomach and with Hilda's help was tying me to the bed. When I realized what they were up to, I struggled to get away, only to be rewarded with a slap in the face that sent my head reeling. My husband used the bell cord for my arms and a ripped sheet to tie my legs. I was spread-eagled, immobile, powerless, vulnerable, terrified!

'The first blow was on my right buttock cheek, the second on the left! A third, a fourth . . . each delivered in a stinging rhythmic sequence! He was slapping me with open hand, spanking his recalcitrant wife! To what end? What had I done to deserve such horrible and brutal treatment from the man who had, only a week ago, promised to love, honour, and cherish me? Had he fulfilled that vow, I would have done anything to give him pleasure. I would have been joyfully his. My body and all its orifices would have been his to do with as he pleased . . . anything!

'I fought back a howl of pain. My bottom was now a hillock of raw, hot flesh, each slap, a red-hot poker! But despite that I was determined not to give in to this hateful man, to show weakness . . . but I could do nothing about the involuntary moans, nothing to stem the flow of tears.

122

'Two questing hands burrowed beneath me to cup my breasts. "Ah, her arse is so plump, so tight – I love the sound of it," said Hilda. She pinched my nipples, at first gently, but then harder and harder, pulling on them, twisting them brutally between her fingers. I writhed to her touch. The sensation, compared to the burning agony of my bottom, was almost . . . (could it be?) . . . pleasurable! 'Twas strange. Even though lost in an anguish of suffering, I was nevertheless aware of the weird and disturbing contradiction. It was as if I possessed two bodies, each in its way supersensitive, one to pain, the other to pleasure!

'My husband's timing became less regular, the sequence of blows unrhythmic. The uncertainty as to when and on which buttock the next would strike created in me an almost unbearable tension, making it more difficult to steel myself for the next blow, to tense my buttock muscles in anticipation.

'Then quite suddenly the torture came to an end. They loosened my bonds, turned me over onto my back. With my poor, smarting arse rubbing painfully on the bed, they spread-eagled me and bound me again. I opened my eyes to see Hilda's face just inches away.

'Her lips descended on mine. They were soft, strangely comforting. She licked my lips. Then, as they relaxed, she passed her tongue between them. I opened my mouth even further, allowing her access. I greeted her tongue with mine. Then, as a solace to my brutalized body, my battered rump, my degradation, I found myself sucking on Hilda's tongue.

'Moments later, the comfort of her lips and tongue were gone, pulled from me brutally by my horrid husband. His voice was a wolflike growl. "Her mouth is mine!"

'"May I have her cunt?"

'"Do what you wish."

'With my eyes clamped shut, I felt Hilda slithering down the length of my body. Then, suddenly, my husband's monstrous instrument was at the portal. Again as before, I locked my lips together against the rude intruder.

123

'Even as I steeled myself against the inevitable retribution, a sudden, lascivious sensation gripped my loins! Hilda's mouth was at my quim! The sensation was as nothing I had ever experienced. Instantaneously a warm flush suffused my body. I moaned. 'Twas all my husband required. In a trice his cock filled my mouth. But nothing mattered other than the lascivious sensations building, one upon the other, as Hilda tongued my pussy!

'My husband grasped my head with both hands. Slowly at first, with deep groans of appreciation, he began to fuck my mouth. I felt the deep crease under his bulbous cock head pass back and forth over the bed of my tongue.

'Meanwhile Hilda's joyfully fluttering tongue had found the small pink cuntal bottom that is the special joy of womankind. Until now I had known nothing of it! The acme! The apex of exquisite sensation!

'Even as my husband's cock passed into my throat almost gagging me, I pressed my hips upward, forcing my pussy into Hilda's mouth. My bottom, as if self-powered, was rotating madly, the discomfort of its burning, stinging arsecheeks almost forgotten.

'My moans and cries were stifled by the enormous cock pistoning in and out of my mouth. It seemed to grow bigger with each stroke. Then suddenly its thrusting ceased. It began to throb. The throbbings grew into twitches, the twitches into tremors, the tremors into convulsions!

'My husband groaned mightily, grasped my head head tightly. "I'm cumming!"

'He ejaculated against my tongue. Globs of jism filled my mouth, seeping out of my lips around the tightly clenched mass of his cock.

'"Swallow it, you bitch-whore!"

'I did as I was told, savouring for the first time the bitter sweetness of fresh, hot spunk.

'Hilda's mouth was lost in the pulsating wetness of my pussy. Her tongue lashed my clitoris. I spent explosively,

124

certain that I was dying an exquisite death. 'Twas my first orgasm.

'I won't bore you with the details, but after that, they left me bound whilst they fucked each other. Later Hilda sat on my face so that I might do for her what she had done for me. She then strapped a dildo about her loins: a cunning artificial cock of leather and india rubber with which she fucked me as would a man. My husband relished every minute of it, fucking my mouth again, cumming on my face, my breasts. Then just before he left, he straddled me and, holding his limp prick as if it were a fire hose, peed all over me. 'Twas the final degradation!

'They left me bound and sopping. An hour or so later, Hilda returned to untie me and to tidy up.

'I was in a state of confusion, devastated by the rejection, the pain, the degradation. Totally innocent, I consulted the only friend I had in that establishment – his sister, Elvira. Though I had difficulty finding the explicit words, I told her everything. I should have known better than to do so. She thought me mad, the victim of a dastardly hallucination. Like her horrid brother – my husband – she too condemned me, accusing me of bringing dishonour onto the family. What to do? Where to turn?

'For almost a year, my husband continued to abuse me, flaunting other women, and on two occasions, fucking them in my presence. More than once he took the whip to me and on one occasion, with Hilda's aid, he tied me facedown in order to fuck my poor, virgin anus! 'Twas at the time a most painful entry.

'Then, after a time, I found to my horror that pain and pleasure seemed to be merging! 'Twas a weird phenomenon, blurring the difference between the two. Agony and ecstasy became as one. I found myself torn between desire and self-loathing. Soon I was both dreading and welcoming his visits. I had become a willing slave to his abuse! He would spank me only after I'd begged him. I began experiencing orgasms from the whip! I longed for

125

him to fuck my arse again, and without my asking – I wouldn't have dared – he obliged me. But as time passed, his visits grew rare. My husband was not spending most of his time in London. He would be gone for weeks at a time only to return with an even more bestial attitude.

' 'Twas then I met the man who now sits at the head of this table: Sir Harry Fibbit. It was a hunt weekend. Ah, how I had looked forward to it. Riding to hounds was one of the very few pleasures left me. But my husband forbade my participation. I pleaded, to no avail. He struck me across the face, saying. "Whores do not hunt fox."

'On the appointed day, a lovely one, indeed, I watched from my window as the guests, their red coats brilliant in the autumn sunlight set out. After a bit, I could hear the horn, the distant baying of the hounds. A dark gloom, even worse that that preceeding it, possessed me. Then, quite suddenly, and for the first time since my marriage, I felt angry. It occurred to me that I was naught but an innocent lass, who had done no wrong, committed no deception. I had been accused and convicted of a crime I had not committed and was wedded to a brute who had no conception of the meaning of innocence, of tenderness, of love!

'In a fit of rebellion, I raced to the stables. There was but a single horse left – Prince Damien. A pure Arabian, she had been impossible to break, having thrown almost everyone who had ever mounted her. I saddled her myself and was astride in moments. At first she seemed surprisingly docile. Gently, but firmly, I booted her into a canter. She responded beautifully. But then, as we approached the pack she took the bit and in seconds was out of control!

'Like the wind, Prince Damien bolted through the others as if they wre standing still. I fought valiantly to gain control; a fruitless endeavour. Prince Damien had her head and there was nothing for it! I was aware of the rage on my husband's face as for a moment we were neck and neck. Then I passed him and raced into the wood. I hunched

126

forward, ducking beneath tree branches that threatened to unseat me, my only hope that the runaway would tire.

'Then quite suddenly, another horse was beside us, matching our stride. Atop it, hunched forward like myself, was a house guest, the young Harry Fibbit, the same as sits now at the head of this table. In a trice, he reached for my bridle, yanked hard, turning Prince Damien's head sharply. The crazed animal reared . . . once, twice. On the third, I was thrown.

'A moment later Harry Fibbit was kneeling beside me. I threw my arms around him in a confusion of gratitude and relief. At that moment, my husband rode into the glen.

' "How dare you, sir!" he cried. "Unhand my wife." My husband dismounted, strode forward, and grasping my arm, pulled me erect. I was no sooner on my feet than he slapped me brutally across the face. Once again I was on the ground.

'It was from this point of view that I tearfully observed the proceedings that were to change my life, Harry Fibbit accused my husband of being a brute. My husband removed his glove and struck his accuser across the face.

'The duel was fought the following evening. Pistols. Harry told me later that he had no experience at swordplay and was not a particularly good shot. He chose pistols solely on the grounds that it would probably result on his part in somewhat less mutilation and a quicker death. My husband, I knew to be superbly talented in both activities.

'The evening of the duel, women being banned from the "field of honour," I secreted myself behind a tree. The two participants consulted with their seconds, then, back to back, paced off the traditional twenty paces. They turned to face one another. Harry Fibbit stood, duelling piece at his side as my husband took careful aim. With my heart in my mouth, I silently urged Harry to raise his pistol . . . to no avail. The fool was offering himself up as a static target! The sound of the shot, no more then a pop, from the ancient, muzzle-loading duelling pistol seemed a thunderclap. Harry Fibbit winced, then stood perfectly still, taking no note of the blood oozing into the ripped fabric covering his left arm.

'Then slowly he raised his pistol and leisurely took careful aim. He held it thusly for what seemed a long time . . . many seconds. Finally, my husband called out. "Shoot man! What in hell are you waiting for?" Harry Fibbit, his arm out-stretched, his piece pointing unerringly at his opponent's midsection, wavered not an inch. More seconds went by. My husband turned sideways, thus making a less formidable target. Still Harry Fibbit refrained from squeezing the trigger. The suspense had me faint. Unmindful of what I was doing, I stepped from behind the tree.

'Since I was slightly to the rear of Harry Fibbit, he was not aware of my presence. But my husband saw me. He stared, a look of consummate fear distorting the usual arrogant cast of his features.

'He turned away from me abruptly. "Shoot, dammit! Why don't you shoot?"

'Harry Fibbit, his eyes squinting down the short barrel of his ornate duelling pistol, moved not a muscle. My husband's rigid stance seemed to collapse. His shoulders sank forward, his body went limp, I thought him about to drop to the ground. "No, don't," he said quietly. "Don't shoot . . . please." He raised both hands as if surrendering to an enemy. As he did so Harry Fibbit brought his gun up, pointing it at the heavens. The shot seemed even louder than that which had preceded.

'I raced to him. His left arm was saturated with blood. Quickly, I removed my blouse, ripped it in half, and used it to bind his wound.

'Less than an hour later, Harry Fibbit and I were on our way to London. Three days after that we were ensconced in a villa in Monte Carlo. 'Twas that night that I first experienced the joys of love.' Lady Doris looked down the length of the table at her husband, 'Ah, Harry,' she said, 'you were magnificent!'

'Bravo!' The table broke out in spontaneous applause.

Dr Hockenbusch said, 'Surely you understand that it is common for innocent young girls to lose their maidenheads – their hymens – from an excess of equestrian activity?'

'Yes,' said Lady Doris. 'That was explained to me sometime afterwards.'

'And what happened to your husband, Jeremy Gordon?'

'With his father's influence he was able to obtain a divorce on grounds of adultery. At first it was disconcerting to be the object of scandal, but soon after Sir Harry and I were wed, the word *adultery* took on another meaning. It became a joyful vice, the pleasures of which we were pleased to share with our friends.'

'Here, here!'

'Under the circumstances,' said Mr Stubbs. 'it would be interesting to hear next from Sir Harry.'

'Here, here!'

'If you insist,' said Sir Harry. He paused as the servants poured the coffee. 'My story is a short one, though hardly dull. I was not quite twenty-one years of age. The charming and beautiful young lady had no inkling of the fact that it was my first time. Fooling her into believing she was bedding an experienced man, however, turned out to be a quite difficult undertaking.

'In case you're wondering as to the reason for my subterfuge, allow me to state that I had reason to believe the lady's one previous experience in the art of love had been a brutal and unsatisfying one. Surely, in the light of that, she would have little confidence in a young man as ignorant of the act as was she. I felt it better for her if I posed as an experienced lover; gentle, knowing, confident.

'Of course, I was none of these. My education had been limited to occasional voyeurism. And yet, by demonstrating that the act of love is pleasurable and fulfilling rather than painful and degrading, I meant to rescue this beautiful young lady from the horrid consequences of her earlier experience.'

'A true act of chivalry,' said Dr Hochenbusch.

'Lovely,' said Deborah MacDill.

'Here, here!'

'Thank you,' said Sir Harry. 'I am quite flattered, as chivalry is a male attribute I value highly. But to get on with it: I realized that I had taken on an enormous responsibility for someone as unpractised as myself. What if I failed?

'At the moment of truth I found that actual participation with one's own woman is a far cry from masturbating surreptitiously to the lascivious acts of others as seen through the narrow eyepiece of a long brass telescope. Here, virtually at my fingertips, for the first time, was a real-life, naked woman! What to do! I had never even kissed a woman in passion before. Could I do any of it properly? How did one begin? And what, if out of ignorance, I caused her pain?

'She lay before me, defenceless, here eyes closed; her body, a voluptuous geometry of curving S shapes, each merging exquisitely into the other. Her scent was a fragrant aphrodisiac that had my head spinning. I thrilled to the sight of her breasts, her hips flaring so gloriously from a tiny waist, her plump but firm buttocks . . . dare I touch? If so, what to touch first? Where does one start? If I erred, would she lose interest? Would she get up, put on her clothes, and leave? For what seemed like minutes I forgot to breathe.

'I had to get hold of myself. I was a man and I must act like one. First things first . . . the initial requirement was that my pego be erect. It wasn't. Why not? It had always, in the past, come erect at the slightest provocation . . . and quite often with no provocation at all! Its will now seemed at odds with mine. Was I not the master? Was I to be done in by a traitorous, ungrateful organ? Damnation! Should not a man have control over the accoutrements of his own body!

'But what to do? Could I stuff it in despite its limp state? Fortunately, I discarded the idea as being wholly amateurish. But I must take some action before she became aware that something was amiss! What?

'Breathing deeply to calm myself, I forced my mind's eye to harken back to the windows into which I'd peered. There were, I recalled, other things one could do! In seconds I catalogued them. Then, fighting to keep my thinking processes active, I bent forward to attempt the first on my list. I kissed her breasts. The action elicited a moan. *Pain or pleasure*? Gingerly, I attempted it again. This time she sighed and laid her hand atop my head. *Pleasure*!

'Thus encouraged, I went a step further. Taking the lovely pink protuberance of her nipple between my lips, I sucked gently. "Oh Harry," she whispered. "That's lovely."

'I continued thusly for a while, at the same time running my hands lightly over her smooth flanks – gaining confidence. My lady responded with a series of little groans, whimpers, and tremblings. Success breeds even more success. I experimented with my tongue, eliciting further pleasurable reaction. Onward! My fear of failure was evaporating. I strayed southward, inserted my tongue into her navel. My lady's increasing response indicated that I was indeed on the right track.

'As I progressed it occurred to me that my lascivious actions had become something more than just a means to divert attention from my flaccid and therefore useless organ. I was creating pleasure in the body of a woman for whom I had the tenderest feelings. 'Twas indeed an act of love from which I too was taking pleasure. But more than that: my feeling of confidence was being transformed into one of power, a kind of erotic power with which I was able to control the very intensity of my lady's pleasure! Ah, I realized, the power to give pleasure was just as pleasurable as the ability to receive it. Though unschooled, as yet, in the more subtle manifestations of the art, I was learning with what I took to be astonishing rapidity.

131

'Onward! With my hands now caressing her breasts, I continued downward till at last my cheek rested on a soft pillow of gossamer hair. I paused, once again calling forth a page from my voyeuristic catalogue. Ah, thought I, here indeed, was a challenge!

'Gently, I spread my lady's legs. 'Twas a sight for which I was unprepared. I'm sure, in thinking back, that I expected nothing more that just a simple opening, a neat circular aperture. What greeted me was, of course, much more complicated. I recall that my first startled impression was that of a flower, a strange and exotic orchid! I have, over the years, modified that initial impression – indeed, reversed it. Now it is the orchid that reminds me of the shrine rather than the other way about.'

Mr Stubbs raised his glass. 'A toast to that sacred, ambrosial shrine before which all real men bow!'

The gentlemen stood. It was a solemn toast ending with six glasses being hurled into the fireplace.

'I was but inches away,' continued Sir Harry. ' 'Twas in for a penny, in for a pound. With no further hesitation, I lowered my head, bringing my lips into contact with the soft, aromatic flesh, kissing as one might kiss more convential lips. My lady's response was immediate. She twitched, trembled, rotated her bottom. "Ah Harry, what are you doing?" By way of an answer, I explored the juicy flesh with a questing tongue, lapped the full length, fluttered into the soft folds, probed the quivering orifice. "Ohhh, Harry, I've never dreamed of such sensations!"

'It was then I realized my once traitorous pego had finally recognized its duty and grown rigid. Harder, stronger, bigger, I felt, than ever before – a tool of iron, capable of any task laid before it!'

'A toast,' cried Mrs Carnaby. 'To that most superb of weapons, the erect penis!'

'Which all real women crave!' added Lady Doris.

'And even, at times, envy!' said Mademoiselle Chartreuse.

'And here's to the warriors who wield it well!' said I.

The ladies stood and, like the gentlemen before them, drank a solemn toast. Their glasses too were shattered in the fireplace.

Sir Harry continued. 'I raised myself up, hovered over her, my weapon at the ready. 'Twas merely a matter of proper aim. Ah . . . it slipped in so easily! 'Twas as if that tumescent part of me had finally found its home. The soft, succulent sheath grasped tightly, sucking me slowly inward. Deeper . . . deeper . . . is there anything comparable to that initial engulfment, that first equisite penetration?'

'Nothing compares!' cried Deborah MacDill.

'It is,' said Mademoiselle Chartreuse. 'the most beauiful of all the moments of love.'

'Here, here!'

'On my elbows, so as not to weigh her down,' continued Sir Harry, 'I advanced, millimetre by millimetre. Finally, when buried to the hilt, her legs locked about me, pulling my body down to hers. As one, we lay in ecstatic embrace; a deliciously quiescent tableau of love, orchestrated by a soft duet of endearments, sighs, and little quiverings. Our lips joined, our fluttering tongues communicated growing passion. 'Twas then I became aware of the subtlest of rhythmic squeezings; exquisite contractions that grew in vigour, clutching and unclutching. I responded by flexing my tool, twitching deep inside her. Except for this silent but voluptuous conversation, our bodies, joined together as if one, moved not at all.

'After minutes, I pulled back slowly, withdrawing almost all the way out of the tight but supple sheath. My lady whimpered. For both of us, the thrill of exiting was almost as great as that of entering. Finally, with only the bulbous head of my turgid organ implanted, I removed my lips from hers and once again raised myself onto my elbows. Then with our eyes locked in amorous stare, I plunged into her! My swollen gonads slapped against her buttocks . . . deep . . .deep! Squealing in ecstasy, her

133

bottom began to rotate wildly! Again, I withdrew . . . again, I plunged! Twice . . . thrice! Each stroke was executed with increased gusto as she thrust upward to meet it. On the fourth I was near bursting. On the fifth I burst!

'I spurted into her, filling her with the thick serum of my love! Lost in a wildfire of sensations, I spasmed again and again as she convulsed beneath me. Once more she held me tightly to her, until finally our only movements were the talented, milking contractions of her secret inner muscles.

'We lay quiet. My pego, now soft, but still firmly ensconced, wallowed in its own juice. Soon, I became aware of a slow, almost imperceptible rhythmic movement of my lady's hips. I responded in like fashion and soon, in a matter of just minutes, my tool was hardened once again.

'We spoke not a word but rather communicated with little flutterings, squeezes, strokings, and kisses. Then I found myself being rolled over onto my back. 'Twas now my lovely partner who was astride; she the rider, I the mount. With a lascivious smile, she began to rotate her pretty arse about the fulcrum of my prick. We were at it again.

'The rest, gentlemen and ladies, I need not describe in detail, as all of you here are well versed in the art and science of fuckery. Allow me to say only that we continued in one manner or another through the entire night and half the next day. I was delighted to find that there was no further need for me to consult my mental library of voyeuristic images. From then on, I required no guide other than instinct and imagination. But most important, my first attempt had been successful!'

'Oh Harry!' cried Lady Doris. 'A virgin! I never knew till now! You poor dear . . . that heavenly night in Monaco . . . and I thought you to be such an experienced lover!'

Sir Harry grinned, sheepishly. 'Until now, my dear, I was never pledged to speak the truth about it.'

'Ah, then it was you, Lady Doris?' said Mr Aziz.

'Of course.'

'Bravo! Bravo!'

'A toast to Sir Harry,' cried Mr Stubbs. 'The most noble and valiant virgin in all of Britain!'

'In all the world!'

'Here, here!'

'Would the ladies object,' said Sir Harry, 'if the gentlemen had their cigars here at the table instead of in the library?'

'A capital idea, my dear,' said Lady Doris. 'And the ladies will join the gentlemen in brandy.'

The men lit up. The cognac was poured.

I was chosen next.

'I hardly know where to begin,' I said, glancing about the table over the top of my brandy snifter.

'At the beginning, dear girl.'

I paused in thought. The *beginning* was a matter of conjecture. 'First,' said I, 'I must know what constitutes the termination of one's virginity. Be it the loss of one's innocence or the initial penetration?'

'An interesting question,' said Sir Harry. 'I think a parliamentary show of hands is called for.'

The vote was unanamously on the side of *loss of innocence.*' Satisfied, I began. 'I was eighteen years old, the daughter of a Liverpudlian smithy, when I boarded the train in Liverpool that was to take me to a new life. I was going to live with my Aunt Portia in London and be educated.

'Until now I had ventured no further from my father's blacksmith shop than perhaps two or three miles. Now, I was embarked on an exciting adventure that was to lead me to a life I could not even have dreamed of. As for my education, it was to be extensive and was to begin even before I got to London.

'Travelling on the railway was not at all the fright I thought it would be. Till now trains had seemed such noisy, smoking brutes that breathed fire and smoke like

135

diabolical dragons. Here I sat in a cosy parlour on wheels, my bottom comforted by real leather as were the bottoms of the three ladies sharing the compartment with me. Out the window, the countryside sped by at a fearsome pace. I was pleased that the sight of it didn't make me dizzy as I had expected. Meanwhile, I felt every bit the lady esconced snugly in a place of polished wood and leather and fine carpeting. It was all far more elegant than any house in which I'd ever been. I sat back, rested my head on the crisp, linen antimacassar and, mesmerized by the regular clacking of the iron wheels, closed my eyes. The three women sharing my compartment were foreigners. They jibbered and jabbered in a language I had never heard. Despite that, I soon found the conversation intriguing. It was as if they were discussing intimate secrets to which I was not privy.

'But at eighteen I barely spoke my own tongue and had little inkling of anything outside my hitherto limited province. Even love was a mystery, hinted at by little more than an occasional wet spasming in my underdeveloped quim, which from time to time I attempted to quiet with awkward fingers. Such fumblings accomplished little. I was still uneducated as to my secret geography.

'The woman next to me began speaking a charmingly accented English. In my half-wakened state it did not occur to me that I was the object of her words until I felt the light touch of her hand on my knee. "My dear," she was saying, "would you care to share some wine?"

'I opened my eyes on her smiling face. "Please ma'am," said I, hardly knowing whether I meant yes or no. I had never imbibed either wine or anything else. One of the other ladies handed her a glass from an open basket resting on a folding sideboard under the window. Hardly bothering to take her eyes from mine, she poured from a bottle she held in her other hand. "I am," she said, "Madam Kooshay." Handing me the glass, she reached into a small, ornate, beaded purse to pass me a calling card.

In eloquent gothic letters, it read, FEMALE EQUESTRIAN SOCIETY — FOR RECOMMENDED GENTLEMEN-SPORTSMEN OF THE HIGHEST CALIBRE — MADAME KOOSHAY, PROP. There was an address in Highcastle Road.

'"Equestrian?" said I, in my ignorance.

'"Yes, my dear. We are what you English call riding instructors." Then, gesturing about the compartment, she said, "And this is Yvette, and Yvonne, each of us horsewomen extraordinaire." She spoke with a heavy, but at the same time, peculiarly soft accent, which made every word seem like a kiss. "And you, my dear?"

'"Jenny," said I, my voice cracking halfway through.

'"Charming name for a charming girl." she smiled.

'"Thank you, ma'am." Not knowing quite what else to do, I gulped the wine as she poured for the two others and herself. By the time Madam Kooshay had filled the three glasses I had finished mine. She emptied the bottle graciously into my glass.

'"A toast," she said. The ladies raised their glasses. "To Jenny." Blushing, I raised mine. "Prosit!" said she, and this time, aping the others, I sipped rather than gulped.

'In a matter of minutes I was feeling quite fuddled. The compartment rotated slowly on its axis. At first this illusory motion was unsettling. But by the time I had emptied my second glass, I rather enjoyed it, and as the compartment melted around me I relaxed into a deeply luxurious ennui. All of the straight lines and hard angles had vanished from my giddy world. Everything about me had softened: the walls, the ladies, the murmur of voices, the sound of our speeding train . . .

'Then quite suddenly, with a startling "whoosh," it all went pitch black! Feeling a dim panic, I assumed that also to be a function of the unaccustomed wine. But we had merely entered a tunnel.

'I lay back against the seat, closed my eyes to keep out the dark. I no sooner had done so when I felt a presence just inches from my face. Lips possessed mine! A soft but insistent tongue found its way into my mouth! It was a new experience, startling me into immobility. Moments passed before I found the wit to realize that the mouth was sucking mine and the hands that even now had found its way under my skirt were those of a woman!

'My resistance was at best tentative, for with my lips possessed by those of Madame Kooshay, others had taken control of my body. In seconds I was being lowered, gently but firmly, onto the floor.

'The compartment was silent except for the sounds of breath being inhaled and expelled in rapidly increasing cadence. I was dimly aware that the train had come to a halt inside the tunnel.

'There were many hands now. They unfastened my bodice, raised my skirt. Two of them grasped my ankles, spreading wide my legs.

'Lips brushed my bare breast then returned, opening wide to hold captive the pneumatic flesh while a soft female tongue swirled round and round the aureole. Even the thought of resistance was wrenched from my mind as that same tongue, with sudden purpose, flicked my now turgid nipple! I felt rather than heard my own involuntary gasp of rapture as suddenly my senses were bathed in sensations to which I had hitherto been a stranger.

'But more – fingers caressed my naked thighs. As I had that day, as on most others in the summertime, refrained from wearing drawers, there was no encumbrance to the hands that even then were nearing their virginal target. How many hands – two, three? Fifteen delicate lady fingers! But one seemed bolder than the others. The bravest of all, it probed forward, finding its way, an exquisite explorer searching for treasure in a silken forest. My body tensed with expectation and this time it was I who thrust my tongue forward into a soft mouth that sucked on it as if it were a sweetmeat. I was learning my lesson quickly when suddenly the lips on mine were replaced with others. An instant later, not just one, but both my breasts were being sucked.

138

'The intrepid finger was finally home. With feather-light footing, it crawled the length of my mossy glen.

'In seconds the single digit was joined by another that lost itself in the sensitive, dewy folds. I felt myself trembling with expectation, for what, I knew not. But despite my ignorance and lack of experience, instinct informed me that what I assumed to be a pinnacle of pleasure was as nothing compared to the heights that lay ahead. I was spread-eagled in pitch darkness, deliciously vulnerable to the lustful machinations of three heated females!

' 'Twas a carnal feast that went on for . . . I know not how long. I had never dreamed such things were done! Actually, I had not dreamed of much at all, having, until now, little substance with which to construct the dreams. All about me were the deliciously liquid sounds of female lust, the cries and moans and whimpers of joyful women! At one point in the proceedings, even as a lascivious female mouth pressed home between my twitching thighs, I found myself likewise engaged, tasting for the first time that tart but sweet ambrosia that is the female essence.

'Having never experienced it. I knew nothing of spending. When finally possessed by orgasm, I was certain I was dying a most beautiful and welcomed death.

'Resurrection came slowly. Drenched in perspiration, I became aware that the train was moving again. I sighed with fond satisfaction, leaned back against the soft leather. Then quite suddenly we were in the open once more. Green hills stretched gently to the horizon. Beside me, Madam Kooshay, her beauteous head tilted becomingly, was exhaling gentle, ladylike snores. With befuddled eyes, I glanced round the compartment. Yvette, her blond tresses flowing in the breeze, was staring out the open window. Yvonne sat demurely reading a small, elegantly bound book.

'But surely this was impossible! Only minutes, perhaps just seconds ago, one of these ladies had been squatting over my face! The other two had been devouring my breasts! Madam Kooshay herself had been cupping my plump arsecheeks in her long-fingered, elegant hands, her face buried between my twitching thighs! My heart, even then, was still racing from recent exertions! Yet there they were, each now involved in a private pursuit as if nothing of the kind had occurred!

'Had I suffered a strange, momentary brain fever? Or perhaps I had dreamed it all in feverish sleep brought on by the unaccustomed speed of the railway – the rhythmic swaying of the coach? But then why was my bodice unfastened? And why was there still on my tongue a savoury, unmistakable feminine essence?'

I glanced about the table. There were expressions of intense interest on everyone's face. In a quiet voice, I said, 'And that, dear friends, is how I lost my innocence.'

'An extraordinary tale,' said Mr Aziz.

'It is certainly one to set the blood racing,' said Mademoiselle Chartreuse, squirming about in her chair.

'A toast to the British railways!'

'Here, here!'

'Ah, but what of your actual virginity,' said Lady Doris. 'It remained intact?'

'For a while,' said I.

'Well, tell us then . . .'

'We are all ears . . .'

'More than just ears,' said Babette Chartreuse. 'Your story thus far has made me terribly randy.'

'Here, here!'

'You've given us the foreplay, now it's time for the consummation.'

'Here, here!'

'Ah,' said I, 'you specified I speak of my loss of innocence rather than the loss of my virginity.'

'But tell us anyway,' said Lady Doris.

'I was deflowered by a man I loved.'

'A rare privilege . . .'

'Love,' said Rose Carnaby, raising her glass.

'Here, here!'

'Tell us of it, all of it.'

'Oh do!' said Deborah MacDill, her voice hoarse with lustful curiosity, her face flushed. 'I so want to hear how your sweet puss was violated – how he put it in you for the first time. Were you on your back? Were your legs wrapped round him? Or did you kneel before him with your pretty bottom raised so that he might approach you from the rear?'

'Perhaps,' said I, 'it is best if I tell the rest of my story another time. I mean, 'tis always best to leave a little something in reserve and besides, – I'm eager now to hear the others. I'm certain their stories will be at least as randy as my own.'

'If you insist, then so be it,' said Sir Harry. 'But you must promise to relate the remainder of your tale at another sitting.'

'I do,' said I.

Next to be called upon was Mr Stubbs.

'My story,' said he, 'is far shorter, and probably far less entertaining than those previously told.' Mr Stubbs sipped his brandy, drew on his cigar, and continued. 'My father died when I was eighteen. He was an eccentric man who had made his fortune in China opium trade and then settled down to a life of respectability in London and Cornwall. My mother never understood nor did she actually ever approve of either him or his sense of humour. For example, she never reconciled herself to a staff of servants, consisting of South African bushmen, American Indians, and Chinese coolies, none of whom had ever been converted to Christianity. He thought it a fine joke and a comment on British tradition of "service," to have a short, fuzzy-headed, coal-black little man in butler's livery.

'He was a most talented womanizer who, along with everything else, at any given time kept three mistresses. Out of a surprising consideration for my mother's feelings, he managed to keep this from both her and the family, but almost everyone else in London knew of it.

'My father showed great disdain for those whose lives were motivated by a high degree of conventional morality. There were a few such in our family, most notable of whom was his brother Harrison and his brother's wife – my Aunt Emelia. Their only daughter, Charity, was a year older than myself and had been raised in an atmosphere of such rigorous restrictions that it was a miracle she wasn't mad. She was, if the truth be known, quite the contrary. Like a weed that sprouts and grows in a soil that would kill off a lesser breed of flora, Charity had managed to overcome her environment. She possessed a sense of both humour and fitness.

'Over the years, both my father, myself and my two brothers had helped her as best we could. Whenever we could, we smuggled literature into my uncle's home for her edification. Hidden beneath a loose floorboard in her bedroom were Jane Austen, Samuel Johnson, Laurence Sterne, Thackeray, Fielding, Byron, Defoe, Balzac, Dickens, and the Brontë Sisters. Tucked in beneath her matress were twenty or thirty back numbers of *The Tatler* and *The Spectator*. During a family Christmas, my father, in full view of Charity's parents, had made her a gift of *The Decameron* bound into a Bible cover! The following year it was *A Thousand and One Nights* disguised as a prayer book! In both cases my father had the extreme joy of being blessed and heralded as a good Christian by his brother, and sister-in-law.

'My father, bless him, died in 1849. At the will reading it was revealed that he had left half his considerable estate to my mother. The rest was divided equally: a third to myself and my two brothers for our education, a third to be portioned out to our faithful but exotic servants to do with what they might, and a third to my Uncle Harrison.

'The only stipulation applies to my uncle. The will stated that in order for the terms to be carried out, his daughter Charity must choose one of her cousins and lie naked abed with him in total privacy through the course of four nights, to run consecutively.'

'My Aunt Emelia, upon hearing this, fainted dead away. My Uncle Harrison turned white as a sheet and complained of what he termed a deadly heart palpitation. From behind the surreptitious shelter of our hands, Charity, my two brothers, and I grinned at each other. My mother, either because she had become more or less accustomed to my father's idiosyncrasies, or because she was instantly preoccupied with the resultant medical emergencies, reacted not at all.

'The will further stipulated that my uncle had five days in which to decide whether to accept or reject the generous legacy. My brothers and I were informed later by Charity of the course of events.

'According to our dear cousin, her father at first adamantly rejected the will. But after consulting, on the second day, with a solicitor who informed him that there was no legal way to set aside the evil, devil-inspired, stipulation, he began to waver. It required another day for him to formulate a justification.

'"*Through my dear departed brother, God is testing my faith. This fortune is meant to sustain a man — myself — who spends most of his waking hours doing God's work. I have already sacrificed my life to Him and now I am being asked to sacrifice my daughter's . . . a fate even worse than death. He died for our sins, can we do no less? Perhaps, someday my faithful daughter Charity might even be canonized for this act of holy martyrdom.*"

'Charity refused. She made a great show of it, throwing back in her father's face all he had taught her of sin, of the devil's grasp on young women who "stray," and of the horrors that await any female who even for a moment allows herself to contemplate the pleasures of the flesh.

'"But," said her father, "it is not *pleasures* we contemplate, but suffering! Suffering for Jesus as he suffered for us!"

'She took to her bed, as had her mother. But still her father persisted, growing more irrational as the days went

143

on. Finally, on the fifth day – the very last minute – she relented.

'Charity insisted, however, that she could not choose amongst her cousins, but must rely on God's choice. We drew straws and I pulled the short one.

'The following night, Charity and I retired alone to a bedroom in my house. We were both naked. After what seemed to be an interminable period of joyful laughter and horseplay we made love. We continued to do so, in every conceivable configuration, for the entire four days, pausing only for meals! It was marvellous!'

'Marvellous, indeed,' said Mrs Carnaby. 'I do so love stories of come-uppance!'

'Here, here!'

'And two young virgins together,' said Babette Chartreuse. '*Très délicieux*.'

'Ah, but neither one of us were virgins,' said Mr Stubbs.

'But what is the purpose of these tales.'

'True, Sir Harry,' said Mr Stubbs. 'But I have not finished. 'Twas actually Charity who had relieved me of the burden of my virginity three years earlier. I was fifteen at the time. She also serviced each of my brothers in their time.'

'Good Lord!'

'A most admirable young lady!'

'What became of her?'

'About a month after the event, she informed her father that she was with child. He chased her from his house and never saw her from that day to this.'

'Did she have the child?'

'No. She had not actually been with child. 'Twas a lie, served up as to be yet another come-uppance.'

'A most courageous young lady,' said Mrs Carnaby.

'Most certainly,' said Sir Harry. 'But what became of her?'

'She changed her name from Charity Stubbs to Jane Douglas.'

'The famous actress!' said Deborah MacDill.

'None other,' said Mr Stubbs. 'I'm sure you've all seen her on the stage as Portia.'

'A toast to Jane Douglas!'

'Here, here!'

'And to the brilliant and wonderfully eccentric father of Mr Stubbs!'

'Here, here!'

'And to Mr Stubbs!'

'Here, here!'

'One question, Mr Stubbs . . .'

'Yes?'

'The question of Charity's virginity.'

'Ah, yes,' said Mr Stubbs. 'That had been a duty performed much earlier by my father.'

There was a burst of laughter, a massive exhalation of cigar smoke.

Sir Harry said, 'Mademoiselle Chartreuse?'

Babette smiled shyly. Would her story, like her name, prove to be a fabrication? I sipped my brandy and wondered if it really mattered.

'My tale is brief compared to the others.' She spoke in a soft French dialect. 'And some may find the account similar in some respects to that of Mr Stubbs.

'It begins when I was seventeen and my friend Charmaine, who was about to be married, was eighteen. We were both very beautiful.'

'You still are, old girl,' said Mr Stubbs.

'For certain,' said Mr Aziz. 'But what is your age now?'

Mrs Carnaby leaned forward in order to look at him down the length of her nose. A glare of reproach lighted her eyes.

' 'Tis most inelegant and ungentlemanly of you to put such a question to a woman,' said she.

'Forgive me, mademoiselle.'

'I'm twenty,' said Babette. 'But I was much more beautiful at seventeen.'

'One tends to age with the passing years,' said Lady Doris, a wry edge to her voice. 'Please go on, my dear.'

'I must explain that Charmaine and I had been very close and inseparable friends since we were children together. She seemed a sister to me and I to her. There had never been any secrets between us . . . except, as I was to find out, one . . . no two, actually.

'Her fiancé's name was Michael, a handsome young man of good family. It was, as you say, a perfect match. They were terribly in love. It was to be a military wedding on the day of his graduation from St Cyr. I was to be maid of honour.

'Two days before the wedding, Charmaine came to me in tears. She would be, she said, an improper bride.

'"Improper?" I said, wondering of what she was speaking.

'Tears filled Charmaine's eyes. "It is something I've never told you. Oh, I'm so ashamed!"

'"You mean . . .?"

'"Yes."

'"But who? When?"

'"My cousin Ernest."

'"Oh Charmaine, how could you?" I felt the blood rush from my head. "You knew I was in love with him!"

'"I'm truly sorry. Forgive me."

'I stared at her, unable to speak. Though my feelings had not, as yet, been reciprocated, I had been in love with her cousin for over a year. He was also a cadet at St Cyr, a classmate of Michael's – his best friend. In fact, he was to be best man. She had not only betrayed me but she had placed horns on her fiancé's head! I would never have suspected Charmaine of such shocking behaviour.

'In a low-pitched voice, she said, "When Michael and I became officially engaged, it stopped."

'"But how long . . .?"

'"Ernest and I have been doing it since I was thirteen."

'"And I never knew – you never told me. Why?"

146

'"I . . . perhaps I was . . . ashamed."

'"We promised to tell each other everything . . . like sisters."

'"Oh, Babette," she said tearfully. "Last year, when you told me you have fallen in love with Ernest, I felt terrible."

'"But it continued nevertheless, you and Ernest, despite my feelings for him."

'"Yes, but only for five more months. When Michael and I became officially engaged, it stopped." She took my hand in hers. "I'm so sorry. You are the last one I would ever want to deceive! Can you ever forgive me?"

'While Charmaine indulged herself in a fit of sobbing, I remained quiet, awaiting the question I knew would come next. It came quickly.

'"What am I to do?"

'"Do?" said I, in innocent voice. "About what?"

'"Just two nights from now I will be in his bed. Michael is a man like any other, he expects his bride to be a virgin."

'"Are you certain? There may be some men — a few — who feel differently about that sort of thing."

'"I am positive. He speaks glowingly of my innocence and how desirable it makes me."

'"Perhaps the only thing you can do then is to tell him the truth."

'"But how could I? I mean even if I could . . . my Cousin Ernest is his best friend!"

'"Then perhaps you should deny everything, say nothing, and insist that, despite the lack of evidence, you are a virgin."

'"Oh, Babette, I could never pass that test."

'"Ah, I see."

'She turned from me to pace fretfully to the end of the room. As if deep in thought, she stared at the wall. "There is a way," she said. "If you'd be willing to help."

'"Of course."

'"No, it is too much to ask . . ."

'I went to her, placed my hand on her shoulder.

"Charmaine," said I, "we must never hide anything from each other, never again."

'"Then you forgive me?"

'"Yes."

'"But . . ."

'"Ask me what it is you want to ask me. I am your true and loyal friend and will do anything to help you."

'She threw herself into my arms. "Anything?" she said, sobbing.

'"Anything," said I, patting her head.

'She hesitated for just a moment, then with her head buried in my shoulder, she blurted it out. "Would you take my place on the wedding night?"

'"The wedding night?" said I, unsure of her meaning.

'"In Michael's bed . . ."

'It took a bit of time to digest her words. I fell into a chair, looked up at her as she hovered over me. "Charmaine, you couldn't be serious."

'"Quite serious, dearest Babette. As long as you refrain from conversation, he will never know the difference. In bed, in the dark, I've been told that we are all the same to them."

'"But I couldn't . . ."

'"You would lose nothing of importance to you. You've said yourself, in the past, that being a virgin has no meaning for you; that you would never marry a man who insisted on it; that you wanted to be liberated from such primitive traditions; that you wanted a man who would love you for your qualities rather than for a mere shard of meaningless flesh and a few drops of telltale blood; that true love should transcend all of that and—"

'"Perhaps I talked too much."

'"Perhaps, though you've always seemed so committed to the notion."

'"But we could never get by with such a trick!"

'"We could. I've thought about it and I know how we can do it."

148

'Charmaine and I spent another hour discussing it. Finally, I allowed myself to be persuaded.

'The wedding took place at the St Cyr chapel just an hour after the graduation ceremonies. As bride and groom passed under the ceremonial crossed sword, Charmaine, a nervous expression clouding her features, glanced my way. I smiled encouragement.

'That night, having secreted myself in a dressing-room closet in their suite at the Ritz, I waited patiently. Finally, the door was open and Charmaine took my place. Wearing a demure, silk nightdress, I closed both closet door and dressing-room door behind me, crossed the darkened room, and got into bed. Minutes later, in the dim light, I could make out Michael's slim silhouette as he entered the bedroom.

'"Ah," he said, "at last, my beautiful bride." He removed his robe, draped it on the end of the bed. "I'm going to make a woman of you, chérie. I'm sure you will love this as much as you love me. And fear not, I will be gentle, tender, and loving."

'Naked, he got into bed. He hovered over me, pressed his lips to mine: a short-lived kiss. Quite suddenly he shot up, reached under my gown to run his hands across my breasts.

'"Babette!"

Fortunately the single word was delivered in a hoarse whisper. Surprised at his quick perception, I said, "We must speak quietly, dear Michael."

'"*Mon dieu!* What are you doing here!"

'"I thought that would be obvious."

'"It's my wedding night! Where's my bride!"

'"We didn't think you'd notice the difference."

'He was silent for a long moment. "Ah, a girlish prank, I might have known."

'"Perhaps," said I, unable to conjure up another response.

'"And now that you've both had your little joke . . ."

149

'"How could you have recognized me?" I said.

'"How could I have not?"

'"We didn't think you would notice in the dark."

'"Dark of night, light of day, it matters not. Kissing you is like kissing no other woman in France. And your breasts — how could I ever forget their perfection?"

'"How sweet of you to remember."

'"Madness," he whispered. "Where's my bride?"

'"Madness, to be sure," said I. "But delightful madness if we choose to make it so."

'"Then perhaps this is actually more than just a girlish prank. You had better tell me."

'"Why don't you just look on me as a wedding gift, Michael, and get on with it. You can have your bride tomorrow night and all the nights to come." I reached for his pego. It was soft. I held it in my hand, squeezing gently. "And you and I can have some of the afternoons."

'"Damn . . ."

'"It's lovely, Michael. I too would recognize you in the dark."

'"Damn . . ."

'It was getting hard, magically filling my hand. With my other, I grasped his shoulder, pushed him over onto his back.

'"What's all this in aid of? You must tell me, Babette."

'"I'm sure you will find that out for yourself, tomorrow night."

'"Find out what?'

'By way of an answer, I trailed my lips down the length of his body.

'"Please . . ."

'"His weapon stood straight up, fully erect. I licked about the head. He reacted with a reluctant sigh of pleasure.

'One thing led to another as they often do, and soon I was on my hands and knees with Michael about to take me from the rear — a favourite diversion we had shared many times in the past. Just as he was about to enter me, he whispered, "Where is she?"

' "Where is who, Michael?"

' "My bride . . . Charmaine."

'I required a moment to remember. "In the dressing-room closet," said I, dropping my head to the bed and thus elevating my posterior even higher.

'It was a long and memorable wedding night, even if not shared by the bride. At one point I elicited Michael's word that he would never mention to Charmaine that he knew of the subterfuge. In order to do this I had to convince him that on the following night, he would learn of its motivation.

'Charmaine was forced to crouch in the dark closet till dawn. With Michael feigning sleep, I let her out. She was angry for my having overdone it. But when I told her of our "success," she calmed herself enough to thank me.

'The next night, Michael did indeed learn that his wife was not a virgin. But, though he tried, he never learned the identity of the man, his best friend, who, years before, had deflowered his wife. Though angered, he kept both his temper and his promise to me. He was discreet, and Charmaine remains under the impression that her little trick had succeeded and that Michael thought her a "proper" bride. Of course, Charmaine and I remain dear and close friends to this day.'

'But, mademoiselle,' said Mr Aziz, 'your virginity.'

'Oh that . . . Michael had taken it from me three years before.'

'And your affair with him,' said Mrs Carnaby, 'had it gone on all that time?'

'Until my friend Charmaine announced their engagement,' said Babette. 'But then after the wedding night, the affair continued for over a year. It was lovely, we met often, usually in the afternoons at a little hotel just the other side of the Bois de Boulogne.'

'Women!' said Sam Smith.

'Here's to them,' said Mr Stubbs. 'Britain would be the better for it if they ran the foreign office!'

'Here, here!'

The last to speak was Dr Hochenbusch. 'My story is simple,' said the doctor. 'I was raped.'

'A large and powerful woman, no doubt,' said Babette Chartreuse.

'It was not a woman.'

'Delicious!'

'Hardly that, mademoiselle. It was a painful experience perpetrated by a madman. I was sixteen at the time.' Dr Hochenbusch drew on his cigar, holding the smoke till he emptied his brandy glass. 'But perhaps it might be best to start at the beginning.'

'Please do, old chap,' said Sir Harry.

'The villain was my Uncle Max, my father's brother and banking partner. He was a widower, recently remarried to a beautiful woman half his age. The name of my new aunt was Helga. She was the daughter of a prominent Prussian family. Her father had been with Bismarck in St Petersburg and Paris where he functioned as an embassy undersecretary. He is now a powerful figure in Bismarck's imperial cabinet. The marriage was a good one as far as business with the Prussians was concerned. I believe that was its sole purpose.

'I saw quite a bit of Helga and we had become friends. She had taken up the sport of skiing, and being somewhat of an expert, I was entrusted to instruct her and guard her safety on the slopes.

'One day she experienced a rather spectacular fall. I rushed to her, fearful that she might have broken half the bones in her body, but fortunately the only damage was a turned ankle. I bound it up in the lodge and we made our way back to Lucerne. We arrived at her house in the late afternoon. There, Aunt Helga was informed by a servant that her husband was in Zurich on business and would not return till the following evening.

'We took tea and cakes in the library where she complained that the binding on her ankle seemed to have grown tighter. Seated in a high wing-backed chair, she placed her foot on a stool whilst I kneeled on the floor to remove her shoe and loosen the bandage. Her skirt was pulled up almost to the knee. I tried not to notice.

'"Josef," she said, "have you ever had a woman?"

'The question came as a shock. She had before never mentioned such things. I stared down at the floor in order to hide my red face.

'"Surely you can talk to me, I'm your friend. Tell me. Have you?"

'"No," I muttered.

'"Have you ever seen a woman with her clothes off?"

'I pretended not to hear her as I rewrapped the bandage. She was persistent. "Have you, Josef?" She laid a hand on my head.

'"Have I what, Aunt Helga?"

'"Have you ever seen a woman naked?"

'"Undressed?" said I, fighting for time in an attempt to build up courage.

'"Yes."

'"You mean, without clothing?"

'"Precisely."

'I stared resolutely at the floor. "Once."

'"Tell me."

'"It was on a train."

'"Yes?"

'"We were going to Paris. It was a while ago. I was only thirteen."

'"And what happened?"

'"It was late at night. Mother and father were sleeping. There was a door to the adjoining compartment . . . a large keyhole . . . peculiar sounds."

'"What kind of sounds?"

'"Peculiar . . . I couldn't make any of it out too well because of the noise of the train. So I put a glass tumbler to

153

the wall and listened. There was a woman sobbing and a man's voice but he wasn't saying anything, just groans and mutterings. I thought maybe someone was sick or hurt." Tying the bandage, I paused, thinking that I couldn't dare tell her more. One simply doesn't talk about such things with a woman.

'"So you peeped through the keyhole?"

'"Yes."

'"And what did you see?

'It was no use, there was no evading my Aunt Helga when she wanted something. She would draw it out of me, one way or the other. Quietly, I said, "I saw a woman."

'"And?"

'"She was naked – with no clothes."

'"Was she pretty?"

'"Yes."

'"Did you enjoy looking at her?"

'"Yes."

'"Her breasts, her thighs, her buttocks?"

'"Everything."

'"Her motte?"

'"Everything."

'"What was she doing?"

'I felt myself growing bolder. I said, "She was with a man."

'"And?"

'"They were doing it."

'Helga ran her fingers through my hair. It seemed a most intimate caress, causing a tingling sensation at the base of my bollocks.

'In a sweet voice, she asked, "Doing what, Josef?"

'"He was in her . . . I mean his thing. And he was pumping up and down – in and out."

'"Was she enjoying it?"

'"Oh, yes. She was moaning and squealing and wriggling all about." I was speaking with no hesitation now and wondered if I dared look up at her.

' "Lovely," said Helga, her voice strangely hoarse. "And you, were you enjoying it too?"

' "Yes. I'd never seen anyone *doing it* before."

' "And your own thing, was it hard?"

' "Yes." I croaked.

'She was silent for a moment. I could hear her breathing. Finally, she said, ' "And . . . is it hard now?"

'I was struck dumb. All of my recently acquired resolve melted away. I found myself wishing I were somewhere else — even somewhere else in the same room at a safe distance. Impossible. Standing up would be even more embarrassing.

'Her hands reached down to cup my face, tilting it upward. She looked into my eyes. "Answer me, Josef, is it hard, right now?"

'Her face in the soft gaslight was beautiful. Her eyes were wide, her lips wet.

' "Is it?"

' "Yes," I blurted out the words.

' "How sweet."

'I turned my head away. With her hands on my cheeks, she turned it back. Then, looking down at me as I squatted at her feet, she spoke with a soulful smile. "Dear Josef, there is no reason to be embarrassed. When a man is hard in the presence of a woman, it is a compliment to her beauty."

' "It is?"

' "Yes. Creating erections is a proud function of feminine charm."

' "You are very charming."

' "Thank you, Josef. Would you like to kiss me?"

' "Yes."

' "Would you like to see my naked body?"

'Once again I was struck dumb.

' "Would you?"

' " "Yes . . ." I thought my heart about to stop.

' "Would you like to touch it, to kiss it . . . my breasts . . . my thighs . . . my—"

' "Yes!"

155

' "Would you like me to be your teacher?"

' "Oh, yes!"

'I stood, unembarrassed now by the bulge in my trousers. Impulsively, I pressed my lips tightly against hers. With her hands on my shoulders, she pushed me back.

'Her voice was low-pitched, with a husky quality that sent shivers up my spine. "Time for your first lesson," she said, running soft fingers across my cheek. "You must be gentle, tender. Take your time. We are not running a race. Women, dear Josef, prefer to be aroused gradually." She placed an index finger in her mouth then withdrew it slowly. With her eyes on mine, she ran it gently across my lips. "Isn't that lovely."

"Yes."

"Now close your eyes . . . good . . . part your lips . . . ah, but not quite so much . . . lovely . . ."

'I waited with baited breath for the touch of her lips on mine. 'Twas a vain wait. Suddenly, with no warning, her hand was pressed against my bulging pego! My body twitched in astonishment. Surely this was a product of my befuddled brain, the result of a sudden overwhelming brain fever! But *no* . . . a quick downward glance verified it. Aunt Helga's graceful hand was indeed cupped over my throbbing organ! Even as I watched, her hand began a slow circular movement. I felt close to fainting. Ecstatic tremors shot through me.

'Helga spoke in a whisper.   "Does it feel good, Josef?"

'Unable to catch my breath, I nodded. With her hand still in place, she pulled me down till I was seated, like a child, in her lap.

' "Close your eyes again, my sweet."

'I complied, aware now that my hips were rotating in tight little circles, thrusting my pego into her amorous hand. I felt a soft tongue licking my lips. Recalling her earlier admonition, I parted them slightly. The insistent lingual appendage sought entry as our lips met in gentle contact. Ah, how soft it was! A shiver passed through my body. Her tongue fluttered against mine.

'Through the rough fabric of my trousers I could feel her hand growing more insistent. "Poor boy," she said, speaking into my mouth. "Your thing is all bunched up. It must be terribly uncomfortable." Exploring fingers traced the outlines of my constricted pego. "It's in your trouser leg, facing the wrong way — downward. We must make it right, mustn't we?"

'"Mmmm," I muttered, sucking her tongue back into my mouth.

'Blindly, she loosened my belt, undid some of my trouser buttons. I felt her hand slip inside to contact bare flesh. The questing fingers descended into tangled pubic hair . . . I quivered with expectation. Never, not even in the throes of masturbation, had I fantasized such boldness on the part of a woman. I quivered with expectation. Then suddenly I was in her grip! Her hand was cool on my hot rigid flesh. Manipulating gently within the tight confines of my drawers, she wrestled the iron-hard staff up against my belly.

'"Now isn't that better? More comfortable?" I squirmed about in her lap, groaning as her fingers played about on the sensitive underside. "Ah, it's a lovely one . . . so fat . . . so much smoother than my husband's." Aunt Helga spoke in breathless tones, her feathery fingers stroking the sensitive flesh just beneath the swollen head. "It's twitching, how sweet . . . and oozing . . . Oh, I love the stuff! Spunk!"

'My moans and groans were a rapturous duet with Helga's lustful endearments. She grasped hold and began to frig me! Had I died and gone to heaven? I threw my arms about her. My rump, firmly ensconced in her lap, undulated wildly.

'"Ah, you're going to spend soon, my sweetheart! I'm going to pump it out of you!"

'My pego began to pulsate in counterpoint to the spirited frigging, each stroke increasing the pressure till I felt I might burst! I shuddered, my body writhed, out of control.

157

'"Cum in my hand, dear boy!" Her grip tightened. The pumping slowed, grew more forceful. "Do it . . . cum!"

'My groin detonated in a paroxysm of ecstatic convulsions! One orgasmic discharge followed the next; spurt after spurt of thick jism!

'"Shoot it!" cried Helga. "Fuck! Spunk!"

'I pressed my mouth to hers, fucking her with my tongue even as the strong, rhythmic pulsations diminished into random spasms and finally into piquant twitches and throbbings.

'With my face buried in the soft, fragrant hollow of her neck, Helga held me close. I became aware that my drawers were sodden with thickening semen. I had spent a copious amount, greater indeed than that which was usually brought forth by solitary masturbation.

'"Ah, you darling boy," said Helga, running her fingers through my hair, kissing me lightly, affectionately. "Are you ready for your next lesson?"

'I muttered an assent into the soft flesh of her neck. She toyed with my earlobe for a moment, then said, "You must kneel at my feet again and remove my shoes."

'Being especially gentle with her damaged ankle, I did as she asked. Then, as I looked up at her for further instructions, a dark curtain descended over my head! 'Twas her skirt and petticoats! Even as I recovered from the surprise, her legs came together, trapping me gently between her knees.

'Her voice was muffled through layers of silk. "Is it not dark and mysterious under there, Josef?"

'I breathed deeply, savouring, for the first time, the subtle and secret scent of femininity. "Yes," I said, my head spinning. "'Tis lovely."

'"It is time you apprised yourself of female geography." Her knees relaxed, freeing me. "You must, dear nephew, think of yourself as an explorer."

'Tentatively, at first, but then with increasing boldness, I ran my hands up her calves, over her knees, and onto the

158

smooth skin atop her legs. The flesh was different from mine; firm, though somehow much softer. 'Twas of flawless texture, lacking the hair, the bumps, the muscular protrusions and rough imperfections of my own. The inside of her thighs were even more so; plump, resilient girlflesh . . . heavenly! I became aware that once again my pego had stiffened. It lay up against my belly where she had left it, trapped in a congealing viscosity within my drawers.

'With my cheek resting against the softness of her thigh, my sensitive fingertips walked the naked *S* curve of Helga's hips and waist, the gently swelling surface of her belly, the dimple of her navel. Joyfully, I roamed an invisible landscape, discovering the true nature of unfamiliar valleys, plains, and hillocks.

'Despite the increasingly intrepid nature of this, my first such expedition, I avoided dealing with the ultimate enigma: the secret orifice that I knew lay at the juncture of my lady's thighs. 'Twas a matter of courage. I steeled myself. Was I fearless man or timid boy? What, I conjectured, if Burton had turned off the road to Mecca? If Cook had sailed past the Sandwich Islands? If Speke had dismissed the possibility of Victoria Nyanza being the true source of the Nile? Was I not also an explorer worth his salt?

'In the darkness I made my decision. I freed my right hand, gave it its head. Then, atingle with expectation, I ceased all other digital activity as it wended its way toward the mysterious apex.

'My first contact was a total surprise. I expected something much different from what I found. Instead of a smooth, delicately fleshed mount, sporting a clearly defined and conveniently placed opening, my fingers encountered a moist complication.

'Helga responded to my first, tentative contact with the juicy complexity between her thighs with a low-throated groan. I was pleased and delighted to find that my exploration induced pleasure. From inside the lascivious tentlike enclosure, I could hear moans of appreciation as her body squirmed about the fulcrum of my questing fingers.

'I roamed about, till finally, at the northern end of the voluptuous forest, I stumbled on an interesting protuberance. As I touched it a tiny, penislike organ emerged from its protective sheath. Aunt Helga's body quivered in response. Encouraged, I passed a gentle, experimental thumb back and forth over its length. 'Twas a manipulation that seemed to engender the most intense reaction thus far. My lady's moans and groans of pleasure turned into squeals of passion as her posterior proceeded to rotate in tight, lustful, little circles.

'In the meanwhile, my forefinger, searching diligently, discovered the elusive orifice. Screwing up my courage, I entered the spongelike tunnel. I hesitated, fearful that I might cause pain, but as if to accommodate the intruder it opened magically before me. I pressed forward gingerly to the first knuckle.'

'"Ah you devil!" cried Helga. As if timed by some lewd metronome, her bottom began to thrust rhythmically with each rotation. 'Twas a complex movement that in a trice swallowed my finger to the third knuckle! Fully inserted, I placed my palm tightly against her groin, wriggling my forefinger deep inside whilst my thumb continued diddling the magical nubbin far to the north.

'Fuck me with it.' Her voice now was husky, low-keyed, barely discernible through the layers of fabric.

'"What?" I asked, confused by her terminology.

'"Your finger . . . in and out . . ."

'Releasing my grip, I obliged her, permitting her to ride the intrusive digit . . . in and out . . . in and out . . . each outward thrust marked by a voluptuous contraction that grasped my finger as if loath to part with it. I wondered briefly how such a tight orifice could possibly accommodate the bulk of my stiffened penis. With an ecstatic chill of expectation, I realized that such conjecture was premature; the question would surely be answered before the day was out!

'The lustful tent grew warmer, more humid, as that part of my lady, enclosed in its confines, began to twitch and jerk uncontrollably. Then suddenly her body seemed a passionate, runaway engine gone berserk! Her internal contractions grew stronger, wildly milking my finger! I inserted two more, "fucking" her madly with them.

'"Fuck! Cunt! Cock!" Her thighs came together, locking my hand in place. "Oh, you dear, dear boy . . . I'm spending!"

'My pego twitched and throbbed in sympathy with her joy. I felt a rush of manly pride with the realization of what I had achieved through the use of just thumb and fore-finger!

'Helga was still. Her legs relaxed as slowly, my lustful duty executed, I withdrew my hand. I peeped out from under the tent of her skirt and petticoats. She lay back in her chair, breathing deeply.

'"Josef, you are developing a deep understanding of female anatomy," said she, breathlessly. "There are men who have been at it for decades who lack the knowledge you have gained in just minutes. You have a natural talent and inclination for the needs and desires of women. You will go far."

'Holding up my trousers with one hand, I stood, gazing down at the beautiful and experienced woman I had just pleasured. Her compliment verified that my baptism by fire had been a success! I was well on my way to becoming a man; only a single hurdle remained. With as much authority as I could muster, I said, "And when is the next lesson to be, Helga?"

'"Ah, my brilliant student is eager to get on with it."

'Quietly, I said, "Is it time for us to remove our clothing?"

'"You want to see me naked?"

'"Yes."

' "You want me to teach you how to fuck?"

' "Yes."

' "My, my. What happened to my shy, reluctant nephew who was crouched at my feet just an hour ago?" She looked up at me, a lovely smile brightening her face. "Has he become a man?"

'Despite my new feeling about myself, I blushed. "Not quite," I said.

' "Then we must finish the job, mustn't we?" She reached out for my hands. As I extended them my trousers fell. She laughed as I helped her to her feet. "It seems you are indeed ready for the next lesson."

' "Yes," said I, grinning with embarrassment but making no effort to pull up my trousers.

' "I am ready too, dear Josef." Brazenly, she pulled down my sperm-stained drawers to grasp my stiffened pego. She pressed her body against mine. Our kiss seemed to last for minutes whilst her hand, locked between our bodies, frigged me slowly.

'Then her back was to me and I was fumbling with hooks. Eventually the dress lay about her feet, and under her precise instructions, I proceeded to unlace her corset. The chore took many minutes. There were also three petticoats, a chemise, and a chemisette. (In thinking about it now, I realize that she must have removed her calf-length drawers hours earlier.) All together, there seemed to have been a hundred eyelets, hooks, laces, buttons, and ties!

'Helga was finally nude . . . as was I.' Dr Hochenbusch drew on his cigar. 'Of course, it is not for me to describe the sight that greeted me. Each of us seated here has shared the exquisite experience of seeing, for the first time, the object of their lust or affection.'

'Which was it with you, doctor,' said Mrs Carnaby, 'lust or affection?'

'Fortunately, both. I have since found that lust without affection is equivalent to making love with one's shoes on; while on the other hand, affection without lust is often

162

symbolized by the arid, self-defeating conjunction of a dry quim and a semi-erection.'

'Well put . . .'

'Here, here!'

'I'm pleased you all agree with me,' said Dr Hochenbusch. 'But to get on with it: within a matter of seconds after the last of Helga's clothing was removed, I too was naked. She lowered herself to the floor, beckoning me to join her. I must add that as is the case with most libraries, even in Switzerland, this one lacked the convenience of a bed. But 'twas no hardship making do with the somewhat soft texture of an Oriental rug.'

'It seems to me, friend,' said Sam Smith, 'that in your state, you would have made do with a bed of nails.'

'That's true,' said Dr Hochenbusch. 'Helga had me in a state of randiness beyond all reason.'

'Truly a most talented woman,' said Lady Doris.

'I've had none since, madam, who was more so.' The doctor leaned forward, resting his arms on the table, his massive head almost lost in a veritable cumulus of cigar smoke. He spoke slowly, his tones quietly introspective. 'I kissed her breasts, learned of the nipple's subtle sensitivities, both hers and mine. In a fit of passion, she introduced me to the joys of fellatio, causing me to spend for a second time. This was followed by a lesson in the art of cunnilingus. I must admit that my first experience at this sophisticated diversion was somewhat amateurish — even, perhaps, a bit reluctant. As we all know, it is an accquired taste. These days, I don't think I could live without it any more than I could live without oysters or brandy.

'Finally, there came a time when Helga smiled at me and said, "And now, Josef . . . the final lesson."

'I was instructed to lie on my back. She straddled me. 'Twas an excellent position from which a neophyte could observe everything. I watched fascinated, my breath stilled. Every muscle in my body seemed acquiver with lustful expectation as she grasped my tumescent, but still virgin weapon. She manipulated it deftly, sliding the bulbous head back and forth along her juicy trench, lubricating it for the final plunge.

'I closed my eyes in order to concentrate all tactile senses on the eminent, initial penetration. Even as I did so, her movement ceased. There was a sudden scurrying. In an instant, my pego was released, the pressure of her thighs against my flanks was gone!

'I opened my eyes on a solitary ramrod pointing straight up from my groin – unattended! Helga had disappeared! Totally befuddled by this sudden, magical disembodiment, I glanced about. Her bare feet were planted just a few feet from me. I looked upward to note an expression of abject horror distorting her features!

'"When the cat's away, the mice will play!" It was a strong masculine voice, a deep-throated menace that filled the room like a portentous swell. I shot up, twisted about to find myself staring into a face twisted in repressed rage! He stood across the room, dressed in a long black overcoat. He was topped with a black hat; in one hand his black leather gloves and ebony cane, in the other a small pistol! 'Twas my Uncle Max!

'I fought to reassemble my wits. I'd been caught in the act with my Aunt Helga . . . my uncle's wife! I stood, my one thought to get back into my clothes, to leave, to—

'"Stay exactly where you are," said Uncle Max. "And you too, my dear and faithful wife." He set his cane against the doorjamb and, retaining his grip on the ugly little pistol, removed his hat and coat. I glanced over at Helga. She was sobbing quitely, her face was tear streaked. Both of us remained rooted in place.

'I stood, attempting to will my ridiculously erect penis into flaccidity. As is usually the case, it seemed to have a mind of its own, and remained totally oblivious to the changed circumstances. Though it seemed at peace, I myself was terrified!

'"Now," said my uncle, his voice strangely civil.

"Perhaps what I've seen has been an illusion on my part or maybe a misunderstanding as to what seemed at first obvious. You are my wife and I owe you the right to an explanation."

'"I can't . . .'

'"Ah, but you must, my sweet. For if you don't explain just what it is you've been doing, I will be forced to shoot your young lover. You see, nephew or not, I have every right under the law to do so."

'I looked about, searching for a means of escape. The window! If I leaped up, I might get through it before my uncle could establish an accurate aim. Perhaps he was a poor shot! I tensed my muscles in preparation.

'"No, young Josef, don't attempt it." Uncle Max pointed his pistol at me.

'Somehow, I must have given myself away. I cringed, attempting to make myself into a smaller target.

'"This is a derringer I'm holding," he said. 'And though it may not be too accurate, I'm quite a good shot and understand its idiosyncrasies. There are two barrels, and though I might miss you with the first, I'm certain to get you with the second."

'"Yes, Uncle Max, sir," said I, my voice shaking. No one had ever pointed a gun at me before. It was a frightening and unpleasant experience.

'"Speak, dear wife."

'Helga was sobbing, her words blurred, halting. "I was furthering your nephew's education," she said. "He is a virgin and I thought it my duty to teach him about life. I mean, we weren't actually going to do it. I was simply showing him a position one might assume. You see, I believe it important for a young man to know about such things so that when the time comes he will not make a fool of himself!"

'"Magnificent! The Baron von Munchausen could learn much from you!" His short, staccato laugh conveyed a sense of nasty menace. I was almost certain my life was about to end. And I was so young! I had never even known the joys of a woman . . . well, not fully.

' "But, joking aside, I can see now that I was mistaken, my dear."

' "Oh dear husband," said Aunt Helga, in breathless voice. "You believe me!"

' "Indeed I do," said Uncle Max. "You must forgive me for assuming that your motives might be less than pure."

' "I knew you'd understand."

' "Of course I do, my sweet." As he spoke, Uncle Max loosened his trousers. "You see, I too believe that education is essential."

' "But then, what are you doing?"

' "Your efforts on behalf of our nephew are, to say the least, laudable. I intend to join you in your efforts. 'Tis the least I can do for dear Josef. As an attentive scholar, he will thus learn valuable lessons he is not likely to forget." His trousers dropped to the floor, exposing long, red drawers. "Isn't that true, Josef?"

' "I'm not sure," said I, a knot of trepidation forming in my belly.

'Helga gasped. "No!"

'Uncle Max fumbled at his crotch. From the sagging red flannel emerged a monstrous bludgeon! My eyes locked onto it in fearful fascination. It was gnarled, lumpish, rough hewn, like the heavy limb of an ancient oak. A pair of intumescent warts punctuated the beveined and be-pimpled horror of its excessive length. The bulbous knob at its head seemed a giant purple tumour. I fought in vain to tear my eyes away from what was surely not the conventional organ of a man, but rather of a rhinoceros, a brontosaurus, a monstrously deformed gorgon! "Please, Uncle," said I, barely able to enunciate the words, "put it away."

' "I intend to do something of that nature, dear nephew." He stepped forward, the horror of his awful instrument bobbing in the air like a conductor's baton.

166

"Now it is time we resume the lesson I so rudely inter-rupted. But first I must mention that I am a strict schoolmaster, perhaps excessively so. Spare the rod and spoil the child is my motto."

'Once again his high-pitched laugh knotted my stomach. "Please, Uncle Max," I said, in croaking tones. "I'll go home and won't say a word to anyone."

'He disregarded my plea. "If either of you disobeys me I will cause a neat hole to appear in Master Josef's skull. It will be quick and decisive. Even in Switzerland, a man's wife, like his house, his furnishings, his livestock, is his property. The state grants me the right to pull the trigger in order to defend its sanctity." With his right hand, he took hold of his monstrous pego to frig it slowly, while with his left he waved the pistol about.

'"Max," said Helga, her voice at once strident and tremulous. "Let him go . . . I promise I will make it up to you."

'"Ah, yes, my little sugarplum, I've no doubt that you'll do that anyway. But enough talk. Assume the position!"

'"What do you mean?"

'"I mean on your hands and knees, bitch goddess!"

'Slowly, fearfully, my Aunt Helga did as she was told. With her elevated bottom just a foot from me I could see clearly the glistening pink furrow. But despite my stubbornly stiff pego, I seemed to have developed a most singular lack of interest.

'"And you, dear nephew," said Uncle Max, "mount her!"

'Mount her? Did he mean astride? Like one mounted a horse? No . . . I knew what he meant. Good Lord, how could I, now?

'He gestured with the derringer and I hastened to attempt to do as I was told. I knelt behind her, grasping her waist. As I did so, Uncle Max was beside me, the gun at my head. With his other hand he grasped my pego and an instant later was guiding it home! I slid in easily; so easily and so quickly that I was in Aunt Helga's quim to the hilt before I realized it. She was wet and open. Groaning, she pressed against me.

'Quite suddenly, Uncle Max was behind me. I turned to stare into the muzzle of his pistol. Behind it he was on his knees, just as were Helga and I. In his other hand: his awful weapon, poised to give battle.

'I spoke quietly in order to give no offence. "I think, Uncle Max, if it makes no different to you, I might prefer a bullet."

'He laughed, causing a wave of nausea to pass through my body. Aunt Helga's hips began, slowly at first, an unexpected, sensuous wriggling. Then my uncle's bludgeon was at the portal!

'"Fuck me, Josef!" she cried.

'I felt no compulsion to do so. I was shocked, depressed, and then terrified at what I took to be her instantaneous transition from abject fear to passion! Then suddenly, none of that mattered as I was overwhelmed in a veritable storm of pain! My uncle's horrendous weapon was forcing its way into the forbidden aperture between my nether cheeks!

'"Stick it in him, Max!" cried Aunt Helga.

'Uncle Max obliged her by driving his diabolic organ in to the hilt. Perhaps it is best if I refrain from describing, in full, the discomfort and pain engendered by this monstrous violation! I doubt I could find the words to do it justice.

'Then it seemed as if a tree trunk were pistoning in and out my poor, unlubricated bunghole! My Aunt Helga's groans joined those of my Uncle Max as she too, in a dastardly act of betrayal, extracted intense pleasure from the degrading double rape. Her plump posterior, in precise rhythmic accompaniment with her husband, rocked back and forth on the involuntary thrustings of my traitorous pego. Suffice it to say that as I was fucked, so was Helga! My pain was transmitted to her as pleasure. Squealing like a madwoman, she propelled herself through a series of orgasms, all the while calling out encouragement to her husband: "Fuck him Max! Up his arse!"

'There were, I admit a few momentary flashes of seemingly contradictory pleasure that surfaced in my sea of agony. And I was hardly aware of spending. But spend I did, as did my horrendous invader, deep inside me.

'When it was over and I had struggled into my clothing, they treated me as if none of it had taken place. They offered me brandy and pleasant small talk, neither of which I accepted. I left the house of my uncle in a blue funk that lasted for weeks. I saw neither of them again, for a month later I was on my way to England and school. When I returned to Switzerland, two years later, they had moved to Berlin.

'But enough . . . for that, ladies and gentleman, is the story of the twofold demise of my virginity. 'Twas, as you no doubt have realized, hardly joyful; a double loss of innocence that was both mentally and physically excruciating.'

'Good Lord!' said Sir Harry. 'She was involved from the beginning! The whole thing was a lewd trap arranged by her and her husband!'

''Twas obviously so,' said Dr Hochenbusch.

'Imagine, using a man in such a degrading and brutal manner,' said Mrs Carnaby. 'It is usually women who are so used.'

'Shocking,' said Mr Stubbs.

'Awful,' said Noel Fibbit.

'Delicious,' said Babette Chartreuse. 'The good doctor was nothing more than a device shared by his Uncle Max and Aunt Helga.'

'Perhaps,' said I. 'But it entailed the sacrifice of a young and naive boy. Despite the benefits to the lady, I find it reprehensible.'

'Thank you, Miss Everleigh,' said the doctor.

'Ah, but don't you agree,' said Mr Aziz, 'that pain and pleasure are often compatible?'

169

'Only, sir, when all parties consent to it.'

'That being the case,' said Sam Smith, 'and please don't get me wrong – I certainly agree with Miss Everleigh – would you consent to such an experience now?'

'With great pleasure,' said the doctor.

'Delicious,' said Mademoiselle Chartreuse.

After a few minutes,' Sir Harry rose from the table to announce that he and Mr Aziz had business to conduct. 'I will join you all,' said he, 'in about an hour in the lounge for what I hope may be a gala evening.' With that he and Mr Aziz left the dining room.

The remaining men retired to the billiard room, leaving the women at the table. It was then that I made my excuses.

I went directly to the foyer, grasped a candle, and entered the walls. A few moments later, I was at the study peephole. Sir Harry and Mr Aziz sat facing one another in wing-backed chairs.

'. . . and it's come to my attention,' Sir Harry was saying, 'that the Prussians, if they can, will betray their Turkish partners.'

'Dastardly!' said Mr Aziz.

'You must guard the shares with your life. Are you armed?'

'No,' said Mr Aziz. 'I'm afraid not.'

'Then I will see to it before you leave.' Exhaling a wreath of cigar smoke, Sir Harry leaned forward. 'The Prussians can manage this without the Turks. You Turks, however, need the Prussians. If they can steal the shares, the Huns will leave the Turks to rot on the limb. If not, then they will continue the partnership as planned. Most important to us is that the Suez shares I went to such trouble to accumulate, end up in Turkish hands. If not, then you and I, my dear Aziz, will not be recompensed for our efforts.'

'I understand.'

'Good.'

'You will travel by rail from London to Venice and thence on the Italian steamship *Triconia* to Constantinople. You leave in three days. At that time I will turn over to you the shares, your tickets, travel expenses, and a pistol small enough to carry on your person at all times.'

I stepped back from the peephole and made my way to my room. What I had heard indicated that it would probably be three days before the Suez shares were removed from the safe. If at that time Sir Harry or Mr Aziz checked the contents of the portfolio, they would find it stuffed with newspapers. But three days gave me adequate time to steal the other half and be gone. In fact just as I had planned earlier, I would break into the safe tonight and be off. The Suez shares would be in the hands of my darling Edward long before they were even missed.

With a feeling of confidence approaching euphoria, I entered my room through its secret trapdoor. I threw myself on the bed, vowing that I would enjoy whatever the evening had in store for me and then, at dawn, I would be on my way from Fanshawe House. The Prince of Wales had made the right choice. He would be proud of me when I handed him and Britain the Suez Canal. Hail Britannia!

I bathed, then took my time dressing. Since it seemed clear to me what lay in store for the rest of the evening, I made use of a rare and lovely French perfume that had been a gift from the Empress Eugénie. 'Twas an exotic scent that existed nowhere in nature – not a floral scent but rather musky and exotic. I dotted it behind my ears, under my breasts, on the inside of my arms and thighs. I wore a dress that could be removed with ease. There was nothing underneath it.

TWELVE

Much like artichokes or Scotch whisky, cunnilingus is an acquired taste. [Samuel Langhorne Clemens]

I glanced about. The American, Sam Smith, was on his back. Deborah MacDill sat astride, a lustful jockey riding an unbroken steed. Her white body golden in the dim light of Japanese lanterns as she rose and fell, impaling herself on the American's mighty organ. Her buttocks slapped against Smith's thighs, her breasts, heavenly melons, heaved with lascivious exertions.

We had been at it for two hours and already I had been fucked thrice and had feasted and been feasted upon. But the evening, I suspected, was still young.

Deborah caught my eye, communicating a rapture so intense that at once I felt I were riding with her! Surely, it was my cush playing hostess to the American's surging zubrik, my breasts that even now were being caressed, the nipples pinched between his powerful fingers!

Mesmerized, I freed myself from Mr Stubbs's embrace. In three short steps I was with her, my lips open to hers. With a fluttering tongue she caressed mine. I reached down, ran my fingers up the length of the deep crevice between her plump, plunging buttocks.

'Jenny,' she moaned into my mouth. 'I have found my true calling!'

'And that is?' said I.

'Cock,' said she. 'I love it!'

'Hard cock?' said I.

'Fat cock!' said she.

'Fucking cock?' said I.

'Yes! Anything! Everything!'

Beneath her, Sam Smith drove upward to meet her downward plunge, driving his stout prick even deeper into her. She gasped as my finger, growing bolder, encircled the secret rosebud nestled deep between her cheeks. I caressed her breast, buried my face in her neck.

'Ah, your finger,' she moaned. 'Put it in me!'

With great delicacy I palmed her buttock, wormed my way in to the first knuckle. I moved it about, slowly.

'Oh Jenny, your finger!' Breathlessly, she rotated her derrière even as it drove up and down, counter to the American's energetic thrustings. 'Fuck ... cunt ... arsehole!'

Soon, with my index finger fully inserted, I could feel, through the thin membrane, Sam Smith's instrument inside her cunt! I pressed against the driving hardness, wiggling my intrusive digit, masturbating both fucker and fuckee! The strange action elicited a deep-throated groan from him followed by a high-pitched squeal from her.

There was a presence behind me. Hands grasped my hips. I spread my legs, raised my bottom to present greater access. An instant later I felt a hot breath on my thighs, then the tentative lap of a soft wet tongue running the length of my open pussy!

Deborah MacDill cried, 'I'm spending!'

'Fuck her!' I called, as my clit twitched to voluptuous lingual exporation. 'Come in her! Fill her with spunk!'

Grasping my finger even tighter, her anus spasmed. Then all motion ceased. Through the sensitive partition I could feel the American's granitic cock throbbing rhythmically, spewing spunk into her, spasm after spasm!

I glanced behind me to discover that the anonymous lover, consuming my now seething puss, was none other than Sir Harry Fibbit. His hands grapsed my undulating

173

derrière, pulling me downward, until losing contact with Deborah, I found myself sitting on his face!

There was an insistent hand on my shoulder. It twisted me about on the fulcrum of Sir Harry Fibbit's probing tongue till I faced his feet. Now, just inches from my lips was a glorious prick – Mr Stubbs's! He looked down on me, his eyes aglow with lust. He was standing, legs apart, straddling Sir Harry's recumbent form. As Mr Stubbs moved even closer, I caressed his beautiful organ with my tongue, exploring the sensitive flesh just under the plump helmet. He hissed with pleasure. Then, making a pillow of my flattened tongue, I drew him in, engulfing him in one deft movement.

Mrs Rose Carnaby took joyful advantage of Sir Harry's prick, which, though blocked from my view by Mr Stubbs's body, I assumed to be pointing skyward. She squatted over it. With her shapely back to me, the intrepid widow lowered herself slowly, engulfing it with a rapturous sigh. Then, much as Deborah had done earlier with Sam Smith, she proceeded to fuck Sir Harry Fibbit, rotating her bum, joyfully screwing herself up and down.

Sir Harry, inspired by this delicious impalement, clasped my clitoris between his lips and whipped it with a rapidly fluttering tongue tip. Inspired by this lascivious lashing, I swallowed Mr Stubbs into the very portals of my throat! Moving my head back and forth, I mouth-fucked him, while beneath me, the talented, sucking Sir Harry plunged a finger into my seething cunt. I twitched and moaned as pleasure pulsed through my body!

At the other end of my cunnilingual champion, Lady Doris Fibbit stood facing the undulating Rose Carnaby, offering her lewd encouragement as the voluptuous Rose rode Sir Harry's cock. Then, raising one leg onto a chair, Lady Doris made her husband's lover a gift of foaming, pink pussy. Rose Carnaby, without a moment's hesitation, buried her face in the succulent nest.

Mr Stubbs was now fucking my mouth as if it were my

cunt. I pressed my lips tightly about the pistoning shaft to aid him in his efforts, as below, Sir Harry was pressing his vibrating tongue tightly against the supersensitive base of my clitoris. There were two fingers inside me now, hooked upward, massaging the secret spot. Shivers radiated out to my breasts, my tightly clasped buttocks, my fingertips, the back of my neck!

Just to my left, young Noel Fibbit, replacing the spent Mr Smith, embraced the writhing, nubile body of his love, Deborah MacDill. With their lips joined, she was masturbating him slowly, running her graceful hand up and down the length of his youthful shaft. Behind her crouched Mademoiselle Babette Chartreuse. The beautiful 'Frenchwoman' was caressing, with one graceful hand, Deborah's breast while the other was busily engaged between her own alabaster thighs.

I thrilled to the lustful huskiness of her voice as Deborah said, 'Noel dearest, I want you to service Mademoiselle Chartreuse.'

'Oh yes, please!' said the lovely Frenchwoman, spreading her legs, her thumb diddling an oversized clitoris as with three plunging fingers she fucked herself. Deborah turned, pressed her lips against Babette's. With her hand still in possession of Noel Fibbit's stiffened prick, she guided the woman down onto the pillows.

'Use me, Master Fibbit,' said Mademoiselle in lilting, French-accented English. 'Fuck me! Suck me! Take whatever you desire – anything!' She twisted about on the Oriental carpet, spreading long stiffened legs, cupping her own breasts. 'Use my body . . . please! Fuck my mouth! Fuck between my breasts! Fuck my bottom . . . Please, use me!'

I watched out of the corner of my eye as Lady Deborah pulled Mademoiselle's legs up and back till knees and shoulders met. The sights and sounds transported me into an even deeper state of lust. With a passionate groan, I pressed the ripe fruit of my pussy tighter into Sir Harry's face.

'Ah, what a lovely little French pussy,' said Deborah MacDill, 'don't you think so, Noel?'

''Tis indeed lovely,' said the young Fibbit, his voice trembling with lustful expectation. I felt a great sympathy, an erotic kinship with the lovely boy as he bent to dip his fingers into Babette's voluptuous swamp. 'Ah, let me taste,' said Deborah, grasping his spunky fingers to suck on them. 'Hmm, spicy,' she said, 'with just a tinge of sweetness.' Thoughtfully, she licked her lips. 'And a lovely, piquant aftertaste. Try it, dear Noel.'

Using both hands, she spread Babette's cunny, revealing a luscious pink. With a deep, heartfelt moan, Noel lowered his head between widespread, welcoming thighs.

A moment later, Deborah's face was next to mine, her lips spread to share in my feast. I withdrew Mr Stubbs's prick from my suctioning mouth and held it for her. She licked the tip tentatively, then took it in her mouth, sucking on the plump head as if it were a ripe plum. Slowly at first, as Mr Stubbs graoned his approval, I masturbated him into Deborah's mouth. Then faster and faster as my left hand, cupping an arse cheek, felt the spasmodic muscular tension.

All the while I ground my pussy into Sir Harry's face, rotating it in small circles about the axis of his magical tongue. His body was heaving as he thrust upward into Mrs Carnaby's redolent quim. Her buttocks slapped his thighs rhythmically. Her delightful squeals were muted in Lady Doris's cuntal bush.

Behind Lady Doris, his arms encircling her, was a resuscitated Samuel Smith. With his hands cupping her breasts, he thrust into her with such force that I, at the far end of the heaving, tempestuous ménage could feel its force as transmitted through the ecstatic bodies of Lady Doris, Rose Carnaby, and Sir Harry Fibbit!

Deborah, now holding Mr Stubbs's cock for me to suck, whispered, breathlessly, 'Somebody is fucking me. Ahhh, Jenny, he's in me all the way . . . a long hard cock . . . 'tis heaven!'

'Who?' I muttered, as Mr Stubbs' stiff penis once again passed between my lips.

Deborah glanced back over her shoulder. ''Tis Dr Hochenbusch. Oh, 'tis so lewd!' She moaned, began masturbating Mr Stubbs as I felt telltale twitches on my cushioning tongue. 'The doctor too is being fucked,' she said, her voice cracking. 'Mr Aziz is behind him, fucking his bum! His prick is up the doctor's arse!'

Though I couldn't see for myself, it was clear that the doctor was indeed reliving the degradation of his youth. 'Twas a lewd and lascivious concept, and for just a moment I marvelled at the foibles of the human mind – would they ever be understood?'

All about were the liquid sounds of joy, punctuated by the rhythmic slapping of flesh on flesh – moans, groans, whimpers, squeals! To my left, Mademoiselle Chartreuse now lay on her back, panting heavily. She was doubled over, her shapely legs about Noel Fibbit's neck as he fucked her with slow but determined strokes. I reached out to caress his shapely buttocks.

Then, as Deborah masturbated him into my mouth, Mr Stubbs's cock, with little warning, exploded! I accepted a mouthful of thick cream, savoured it, then quickly, transferred the spewing organ into Deborah's eager mouth! Caressing his bollocks, I thrilled as his cock twitched uncontrollably. Thick, white nectar dripped from the corner of Deborah's suctioning mouth. Ecstatic, we combined our efforts to lick him clean.

Beneath me, Sir Harry's fingers, his lapping tongue and nibbling teeth was inducing a wildfire of sensations throughout my body. All of me, every passion-whipped part, tingled, fluttered, throbbed. An unbearable, yet exquisite pressure was building . . . building!

Deborah and I spent together, our mouths joined in a spunk-smeared kiss. 'Twas actually an orgasm shared by four of us. Just at its peak, Dr Hochenbusch shot off inside her, as did Mr Aziz in the doctor's clutching anus.

177

There followed in the next few minutes a series of orgasms as Lady Doris gushed to Rose Carnaby's talented tongueing, Sir Harry Fibbit spasmed his seed into Mrs Carnaby, Sam Smith shot into Lady Doris Fibbit's talented quim just as her son Noel spent into her orgasm-racked, adopted daughter – the talented and versatile Mademoiselle Chartreuse.

We rested, drank ice cold champagne, and spoke of cabbages and kings. Then, insatiable, we were at it again. The naked games continued, in every possible combination. I became supersensitive, the slightest touch enough to transport me into shattering orgasm. I was cunt! All of me! An hour before the sun was to rise, I had fucked each of the men at least once – seven or eight doses of luscious spunk combining in my seething pussy!

Finally all of us lay about, on the chairs, the sofas, the floor – exhausted. A fragrant scent of sex filled the atmosphere. There was the sound of whispered conversation, restrained giggling, and the manly snores of Sir Harry Fibbit.

Thirteen

Many, otherwise educated ladies and gentlemen, go through life unaware of the female orgasm. This constitutes a state of ignorance beyond that of the most uncivilized aborigine. [JENNY JEROME (to a friend)]

Many labours in the garden of Eros had exhausted me. Lost in a delicious languor, I lay atop a pile of pillows, lulled by the dulcet snores of Sir Harry, who reposed but a few feet away. Both my mind and body drifted in and out of a cosy stupour unmodified by the tiny nagging imperative that I rise up and get on with it. The study, the safe, the Suez shares; my career as a spy could await my recovery . . . a few minutes, perhaps even a half hour – one was capable of only so much . . .

I awoke to sunlight streaming in the windows. The mantel clock read eight-thirty! Around me, just a few of last night's naked participants lay, sleeping the sleep of the innocent. Gone was Dr Hochenbusch, Rose Carnaby, and the entire Fibbit family: Sir Harry, Lady Doris, Noel, and Mademoiselle Babette.

I shot up, found my dress in a disorganized pile of assorted raiment. Disregarding hooks and laces, I threw it in on and, with shoes in hand, made my way directly to the study.

I opened the door on the unmistakable sounds of fuckery. With heavy drapes drawn against the morning light and an absence of candles, my straining eyes at first

179

communicated the image of a hulking two-headed monster dancing in place in the very centre of the book-lined, walnut-panelled room.

'Ah, Jenny. Good morning to you, my dear.' 'Twas no mistaking the breathless voice of Rose Carnaby.

As I approached, and as my eyes adjusted to the gloom, the monster resolved itself into a standing Starns about whom was draped the figure of Mrs Carnaby. Both were naked. She hung, attached to the tall butler by arms and legs wrapped about him. His hands cupped her buttocks, supporting her, as beneath, his shaft pistoned forcefully, in and out of her accommodating sheath.

Foiled in my attempt to get at the wall safe, I decided to make the best of it. I lit a few candles and settled into a chair to observe the lewd performance.

'Ah, that's lovely, Starns,' said Mrs Carnaby as the butler shifted position in order to allow his cock to enter at a slightly lower angle. She looked down at me, a beatific smile gracing her pleasant face. 'He's marvellous, Jenny . . . ah yes . . . have you tried him yet?'

'I'm afraid not,' said I, warm randiness beginning to creep into my loins.

'You should, my dear,' said she, thrusting her hips back and forth. 'He has a delightfully novel prick, unlike any I have experienced. 'Tis curved upward at a most acute angle.' She paused for a moment, closing her eyes as a wave of pleasure seemed to wash over her. 'Exquisite!' She shuddered, clung tighter to him, squeezing his waist with her shapely legs. He groaned, slowed the pace slightly. 'Ah yes, Jenny dear, a cunningly shaped prick, the only one I've ever had that can reach that secret spot so few of us know about.'

'Indeed,' said I, stretching my legs out and pressing a hand against a feverish quim that even through the heavy material of my dress seemed soft, open, and ready.

'Do you know of it?'

'Of what?' said I.

'The "spot".'

'Yes,' said I. 'I had an Egyptian lover who taught me of it. 'Tis like an internal clitoris.'

'First you feel as if you must pee but then . . . he's doing it to me now. His cock head is rubbing back and forth against it.' She shivered, clamped her eyes shut. 'Ah, how exquisite, it is . . . the nuances . . . I believe I'm about to spend.' Her eyes opened wide to engage mine as her body trembled uncontrollably.

'Lovely,' said I.

'Lovely indeed,' said Rose, endeavouring to control her breathing. 'You should try him.' She paused as yet another momentary spasm of pleasure took hold. 'It's a glorious sensation. I've spent twice in fifteen minutes; a minor miracle, considering that I've been rendered somewhat temporarily insensitive by last night's activities.'

''Tis always the opposite with me.' I lifted my skirt in order to explore with delicate fingers. My clitoris had assumed a hypersensitivity that made the merest contact excruciating.

'Ah, thank you, Starns, it's lovely,' said Rose Carnaby. 'But I do believe I've had about enough.'

'You're welcome, madam.' He lowered her to her feet.

The door opened to admit Deborah MacDill. She was prettily dishevelled, her dress, like mine, thrown on carelessly.

'Good morning, all,' she said, yawning. Then, seeing Starns, she stared for a moment, lowering her eyes to his banana-curved tool glistening in the candlelight. 'Oh, magnificent . . . may I be next, Aunt Rose?'

'No, my dear. You must take your turn. Miss Everleigh is ahead of you.'

I smiled at Deborah. 'I'm in no great hurry. It would be all right if you played through—'

'No,' said Mrs Carnaby. 'Deborah must learn patience.'

'Yes, Aunt Rose.'

I stood as Starns took my hand. In a moment I was out of

181

the dress. Standing behind me, he ran his hands over my dress as if acquainting himself with it.

'I think it best if you stretch out on your back atop the desk, dear Jenny,' said Rose. 'It's an ideal height for Starns and he's quite good in that position.'

'Thank you, Rose,' said I.

'Thank you, madam,' said Starns.

Mrs Carnaby placed a pillow under my derrière, then seated herself on the arm of Deborah's chair. I bent my legs at the knee, spreading them wide in order to expose myself to him. His unusual weapon, curving upward like a rhinoceros horn, bobbed in the air as he approached. He grasped it, stared down at its target. I closed my eyes.

The initial penetration was breathtaking. He went all the way in with one fluid motion of his hips. Then slowly, as I opened my eyes, he proceeded to fuck me. His movements were conducted with measured cadence as if timed by a metronome.

During a brief lifetime of six or seven minutes that followed, our only contact was genital. Not once did either of us remove our eyes from that connection. Nor did we use our hands on each other or utter an expression of passion. Our only sounds were that of breathing. 'Twas pure, lacking all subtlety, all nuance, all fantasy . . . all pretension.

Our only movement was that of his clockworklike hips. Mine were stilled, as was the rest of my body. I moved them, neither voluntarily nor involuntarily. There was no need. The vaunted secret 'spot,' spoken of so eloquently by Rose, played no part, nor did my more obvious clitoris, which remained unstimulated throughout.

My pleasure was derived solely through a strange sense of an increasing 'fullness,' as if somehow I had been miraculously transmuted into a man. Was I the cock and he the cunt? Was it I who was the fucker and he the fuckee? Yes . . . no . . . yes . . .

My orgasm, simultaneous with his, was explosive, but

brief. A second, a millisecond. Then he was out of me and I lay, hating him and somehow devastated to find myself, once again, a woman.

As Deborah assumed the position I had vacated, I dressed. Her squeals of pleasure left me singularly unmoved. I wondered if I would ever enjoy the act again. I nodded to Rose Carnaby as I left. There were no words between us. She looked at me as if somehow she understood.

Once in my room I fought to come to my senses. Should I wait for them to leave the study and then attempt the safe? No. It would be foolhardy. It was already too late in the day. Everyone was up and about now and any one of them might enter the study to borrow a book, to fulfil an assignation, to confer. Once again, it would have to await the night.

Strangely forlorn, I bathed, and foregoing breakfast, threw myself naked across the bed.

I was awakened at noon by Mademoiselle Babette, who was attired in a dressing gown. She presented me with a glass containing a strange-looking reddish liquid. I refused her offer as gracefully as I could. She insisted, explaining that it would 'be good for me and would revive both strength and spirit.' With the realization that if it were a drug it would be disguised in a more familiar libation, I finally complied.

The drink was burning to the tongue but peculiarly refreshing. When I asked her the nature of the contents, she said, 'The juice of tomatoes, pepper, Worcestershire sauce;* all whipped up together along with a bit of this-and-that and a dollop of gin. Lady Doris calls it a Bloody Lady.

* Worcestershire sauce was first compounded in the year 1837 in the borough of Worcester, County Worcestershire. Its original formulation was based on hops, raisins and locally grown spices but over the years, the hops were dispensed with for more exotic contents such as chili peppers and anchovies, etc.) J.E.

Babette informed me of Lady Doris's suggestion that I join her in the 'gym.' I wondered at the invitation, finally recalling that the word *gym* was short for gymnasium. It seemed a most peculiar place for women. In my limited understanding, a gymnasium was a purely masculine habitat where wrestling contests and such like were conducted.

Nevertheless, with a feeling of increased vigour and well-being (obviously engendered by the 'Bloody Lady') I too donned a dressing gown and accompanied my escort below-stairs.

The gym was the place of white tile I had viewed through a peephole and assumed to be some sort of torture chamber. As I entered, Lady Doris greeted me with a wave from the centre of the sunken pool. She wore, on her head, a close-fitting black cap. (I was later to find out that it was made of a kind of india rubber, lined with light canvas. Known as a bath hat or bathing cap, its cunning purpose was to keep one's hair dry.) I watched in amazement as, floating at ease on her side, Lady Doris, much like a human fish, was propelling herself with a graceful and confident motion of legs and arms. I had never seen it done before. My assumption had always been that drowning was the natural consequence of human immersion in deep water and that swimming, far from being an indulgence, was something one attempted only in dire emergency.

Just behind me, on a large grey mat, Sir Harry and Dr Hochenbusch, their muscular bodies glistening with oil, were involved in a bout of Greek wrestling. The young Noel Fibbit was busily running a mindless circuit around the pool. Babette, had stepped out of her dressing gown and was now hanging by her knees from a trapeze! 'Twas indeed a weird mélange, involved in an assortment of activity I found bizarre and to no purpose I could ascertain. The place was after all (as I had originally perceived) a torture chamber. The torture, however, seemed to be of the self-inflicted variety.

Except for Lady Doris's bath hat, the two women were totally nude. The three gentlemen wore nothing but small pouches, the function of which, I assumed, was to prevent their penises from flopping about.

Noel smiled at me broadly as he trotted past on yet another circuit of the pool. I waved to him, then looked down to see Lady Doris, her chin resting on her arms at the pool edge.

'Good afternoon, Jenny,' said she. 'I hope you slept well.'

'Thank you, I did,' said I.

'But then why do I sense a note of consternation?'

'More a note of awe than consternation.'

'Ah, then you're wondering what this is in aid of.'

'Yes,' said I. 'And though I admire the skill and dedication of each of the participants, I must admit it all seems quite pointless.'

'Hardly that,' said Lady Doris. 'If you remove your dressing gown, you can sit here and dangle your feet in the water while I explain it to you.'

I dropped my gown and sat, dunking a tentative toe. The water was not nearly as cold as I feared it to be.

'We heat it,' said Lady Doris. 'I find it enervating when it's too cold, though Sir Harry maintains just the opposite. He could swim with ease amongst the icebergs in the North Atlantic.' She laughed. 'And have no fear, dear Jenny, 'tis quite sanitary, we change the water each week.'

'But what's the purpose of all this,' I asked. 'I can understand the wrestling, it is by way of a contest. But why would one want to swim about, or run circles, or hang from their knees?'

'Exercise.'

'Exercise?' said I. 'Why?'

'Because it's good for you.'

'But how could that be? One only has so much energy, why waste it on useless, debilitating activity?'

'That's what most people believe,' said Lady Doris. 'But

they're mistaken. Exercise tones the kidneys, smooths the skin, dissolves the fat, develops the muscles—'

'Muscles?'

'Yes?'

'What need does a woman have for muscles?'

'For one thing, it is muscles that keep your breasts elevated.' Lady Doris reached up to poke an area between my breasts and shoulders. 'Right here,' she said. 'If you exercise properly, this particular muscle will keep this one pointing heavenward till you are seventy.'

I never imagined such a thing.'

'And more, dear girl. 'Do you recall our first little chat when I told you I might divulge the secret of my youthful appearance?'

'Yes, I've thought of it since,' said I.

'Ah, I'm glad you have.'

'Exercise?'

'That and the food one eats,' said Lady Doris. 'We have been confirming to Dr Hochenbusch's theories for a decade, and as you can see, they've functioned admirably for all of us.' She gestured at the wrestlers, who, locked together in a grotesque tableau, were grunting like animals. 'Where else would you see men of their age involved in such strenuous activity with no ill effects? And furthermore, where else could you find a man of Sir Harry's years capable of functioning so superbly with a woman? You yourself would testify that he is capable of keeping up with men less than half his age.'

'Carrots?'

'And fruits and nuts, not to mention green things; sprouts and so forth.'

'Don't they give one gas?'

'Perhaps, my dear, but if people exercised more they'd fart less.'

'I had no idea.'

'And one must refrain from overeating, which is a difficult discipline indeed, particularly in an age that's devoted to gluttony.'

'Indeed,' said I, thinking that perhaps she wasn't completely mad. In fact I was beginning to believe her, for surely the proof, as they say, was in the pudding; and the pudding, both helpings of it, were almost ideal specimens, despite their age.

'Of course we're not perfect. We do indulge ourselves from time to time, as you've no doubt noticed. And we imbibe a bit more than we should.'

'No one's perfect,' said I, dazzled with the idea that I might age as well as Lady Doris had. There were few beauties in Britain past thirty-five and not too many older than thirty. 'Will you teach me?' said I.

'Of course, my dear.'

For just a moment I realized that tonight I was going to betray this kind and gracious woman and her generous husband. Feeling the sharp sting of guilt, I looked away. Spying could indeed be a dirty business. But how does one choose between love of country and other aspects of civilized behaviour; graciousness, loyalty to friends, respect and love for one's fellow man, simple honesty? I began to realize the reason for my reluctance to accomplish the final deed, the excuses I had made to myself for not getting at the study wall-safe earlier. There seemed to be a part of the mind that shunts aside the unpleasant while at the same time supplying rationalization and diversion. But, of course, I had no other choice. I had made the commitment. Beside the obvious question of patriotism there was also the question of which person to betray. It had to be one or the other. Was it to be Edward or Sir Harry Fibbit?

Lady Doris laid her hand on my arm. 'Jenny dear, are you quite all right?'

'Forgive me, Lady Doris,' said I, managing a smile. 'I was just thinking of something.'

'Now, Jenny, is not the time to think. It is the time for exercise.'

'Let us begin,' said I.

'First, I will teach you to swim. Then after a bit of lunch I will show you a few simple things that along with a certain culinary moderation will keep you young and beautiful for many, many decades.'

Fourteen

Show me a man who appreciates the educated talents of older and experienced women and I'll show you a man who understands pleasure and even the joys of sharing it. Show me a man who doesn't and I'll show you a man whose interest is merely to verify his own questionable virility. [Thomas Carlyle]

That evening, an hour or so after the orgy had begun, I slipped away to make my way to the study. Lighting a single candle, I held it in my left hand whilst with the right I slid the small oil painting upward. The metal safe glistened ominously in the candlelight. Taking a deep breath, I emulated Sir Harry by twisting the dial a few times round to the right, then left to sixteen. Carefully, I rotated right to four then left again to ten. The fourth number was the one I did not possess. I started with the number, one. I repeated the entire process with two, then three, then four. Fortune smiled on me at my eighth attempt. There was a click and the safe was open!

Less than fifteen minutes had passed. Whoever missed me at the orgy was sure to assume that I had gone to answer a call of nature. Nevertheless, anyone could come through the study door; there was no inside lock. Therefore, time was still of the essence. I removed the beribboned roll of stock shares from the safe, leaving the portfolio that I had earlier stuffed with newspapers. I closed the small door, rotated the dial, pulled down the painting.

My plan was to make my way through the walls to my room. Just as my fingers touched the hidden latch on the underside of the wainscoting rail, I felt it move. For an instant the strange mechanical action confused me. Then in a flash, I realized that someone on the other side was operating the latch! I blew out my candle and made for the only possible hiding place within reach – the sofa. As I crawled behind it a soft light pervaded the room. Someone with a lit candle was entering through the secret door! Peering beneath the couch, I could see his feet as he passed. He wore black, highly polished shoes and black trousers. More than that was lost to me.

I was aware of movement at the other end of the room, the sound of the painting sliding up. I fought to calm myself, to think. My alternatives were limited. I must still exit through the walls according to my original plan. To do otherwise would necessitate making my way through the ground floor of the house while carrying the shares. It was dire risk, as I was naked and had no means to conceal them from whomever might be strolling about.

The mysterious stranger let loose a curse. 'Twas a single word, 'Damn!' Not enough for me to recognize his voice, but enough to indicate that it was the Suez shares he was after and that he had found them missing. The sound of the safe door being slammed shut startled me. My skin crawling in fear. Who was he? What would he do if he discovered my presence? Certainly neither of us was in a position to give the hue and cry. Then once again I could see his feet as he passed.

A moment later he was through the secret door. It clicked shut and I was alone in the dark. Feeling my way to the secret entrance, I counted slowly to ten, tripped the hidden latch, and entered the walls.

His candle was a bobbing light in the distance. Having refrained from lighting a candle of my own, I found the dim glow from his to be sufficient to guide my way and to avoid the pitfall of the ladder opening descending to the pantry. It also enabled me to find the ascending ladder that led me to the second floor. From that point on I made my way in total blackness, hugging the wall.

Once in my room, I dressed quickly, then retrieved both the Suez shares and the pistol from where I had hidden them beneath the floorboards. I placed both batches of shares, the pistol, and my purse in a pillowcase. I ripped a strip of material from a sheet to form a rudimentary shoulder strap. The pillowcase would be my only luggage.

Leaving everything else, including a steamer trunk filled with clothing, I went through the door and down the hallway to the back staircase. Three minutes later I was in the stable.

There were three riding horses. In the gloom, I chose a mare and attached bridle and bit. There was no need to take the time to saddle up. As the child of a smithy I was adept at riding astride and bareback. With my makeshift, pillowcase rucksack hanging from my shoulder, I was out of the stable and mounted in just two minutes.

Before I had gone a mile I knew the identity of the mysterious stranger in the study. The knowledge frightened me and I cantered a quarter mile before realizing the foolhardiness of tiring my mount. 'Twas over and despite the last-minute complications I had succeeded in my mission. I was a successful spy. Somehow the thought depressed me, and losing myself in the jogging motion of my horse, I ceased thinking about any of it. After an hour or so a strange, false dawn lit the sky behind me. Was it, I wondered, a portent?

With my mind a blank, I was across the Marsten Moor and within sight of the Driffield railway station a few minutes after the real dawn. Dismounted, I slapped the horse on her rump, sending her back whence she had come. Then I crossed the tracks, making my way a few yards into the dense wood. There I sat up against a tree to await the first southbound train.

It was then that I realized Edward's gift, the ruby

necklace, was still in my room at Fanshawe House. 'Twas the trigger that released my tears. They were tears not for the loss of the necklace but for everything – all of it – the guilt, the fear, the fact that I had lied and stolen from people who had done me no wrong, who had respected and trusted me and who seemed not at all the villains I had expected them to be ... Rule Britannia ... I fell into a fitful sleep.

The arrival of a train awakened me. The position of the sun indicated that I had slept for less than an hour. In order not to be seen by anyone on the platform, I boarded on the blind side, away from the station. The compartment was, fortunately, empty – I could not have borne to share it. As the train moved out of the station I once again fell into a shallow sleep.

It was a head and shoulders silhouetted by the sun outside the window that awakened me. Someone was on the running board! Even though I could not see him clearly, I knew who it was! Aside from the guests at Fanshawe House, all of whom, at the time, were naked, there was only one who would possibly be well turned out in shiny patent leather shoes and black trousers! Before I could arouse myself completely, he was in the compartment, a diabolical knife grasped in his right hand.

'Good morning, Miss Everleigh.'

'Good morning, Starns,' said I, surprised at my own state of calm.

'You know what I'm here for?'

'Yes, and I know why and on whose behalf.'

'You are extremely intelligent and resourceful, for a woman.'

'Twas a backhand compliment. I reciprocated as well as I could. 'And you,' said I, sweetly 'are a superb butler. The role suits you.'

'Now I know,' said Starns, 'that it must have been you behind the wall during my little adventure with the scullery maid.'

'Yes,' said I. 'It took forever for you to get on with it.'

'True,' he said, with a sardonic laugh. 'But if my ears served me right, you took quite an interest in the proceedings.'

Our tones were strangely conversational, considering the circumstances. He grinned and I felt a peculiar relief. At long last I was confronting – or being confronted by – a *genuine* villain. For surely, thought I, anyone working for the horrid Prussians filled that category. Out of a genuine curiosity, I said, 'How did you know I had them?'

'They were missing and so were you. On the pretence of serving champagne I entered the lounge to conduct a little census. You were the only one not present. In fact, Mrs Carnaby asked if I had seen you. I told her I had seen you on the stairs and that you had asked me to tender your regrets but that you had felt a little ill and had gone to bed.'

'Why?'

'Simply, Miss Everleigh, to keep anyone from leaving the room before I could lock the doors. It was merely a simple subterfuge.'

I felt a sudden rush of trepidation. 'Why,' I said, now fighting to continue in calm voice, 'Did you want to keep them all together?'

'Simply because a localized, concentrated conflagration burns much quicker and much hotter than one that has to be spread over a wider area. I made use of tallow and benzene. It was almost instantaneous, as much an explosion as a fire. From a quarter mile away the entire sky seemed lit up. An impressive sight.'

Surely, thought I, he was concocting this monstrous tale in order to coerce me. Quietly, with as much dignity as I could muster, I said, 'An ingenious lie, Starns, but I'm not that easily frightened.'

'My dear Miss Everleigh, I've no reason to lie to you.' His voice was pitched low, the words enunciated precisely through lips locked in the grimace of a smile. 'It matters not, in the scheme of things, whether you believe me or not.'

His eyes, deep, unfathomable, bored into mine, giving the lie to his smile. A winter chill passed through my body freezing all doubt into certainty. 'Good Lord, you murdered them all!'

'I did, indeed, Miss Everleigh. This is a serious business we're engaged in. I never cease being amused at the manner in which you British and your American cousins play at it as if it were a game — a cricket match. You are invariably shocked when faced with the realization that the rest of the world is quite professional and unsporting.'

My mind went numb with horror. He was mad! He had killed them all! Gracious Lady Doris, lovely young Deborah, precocious Babbette, witty Mrs Carnaby, generous Mr Stubbs and the others; all dead! 'Twas monstrous! Battling for my wits, I said, 'Why?'

'So as to conceal my identity. In order to prevent anyone from coming after me in an attempt to retrieve the shares. There are those, in addition to you and I, who will stop at nothing in order to lay hands on them. You see, madam, what you have secreted in that pillowcase beside you is worth more than money. The Suez shares represent tremendous power, they are the key to empire. What are a few insignificant deaths compared to that?'

I breathed deeply in a successful effort to overcome my fear. 'And is mine to be one of those insignificant deaths?'

'I'm afraid so, Miss Everleigh. It will be the part I relish least in this otherwise most satisfactory and exciting affair. I must say that I'm truly sorry . . . such a beautiful woman. A shameful waste. But what am I to do? I promise you, if you don't struggle, I will make sure it is painless and instantenous. Actually, you see, I'm quite good with a knife. Firearms depress me, they are so noisy and not at all reliable.'

He was mad. I glanced at his knife, then reaching into the pillowcase, withdrew the Suez shares. Without a word I threw them at his feet. He smiled and, with his eyes still on me, bent to retrieve them. He was momentarily off balance. It was now or never! In an instant I had the pistol out of the bag. With my finger on the trigger, I pointed it straight at his head!

'Leave them on the floor,' said I, fighting to keep my voice from cracking.

'Ah, Miss Everleigh,' said he, straightening. 'I underestimated you. You are a professional, after all.'

'And,' said I, 'open your right hand.'

He did so. The knife clattered to the floor.

'Who are you?'

'My name is Heinrich Werner von Seydlitz Holstein, at your service, madam. And you?'

'Jenny Everleigh.'

'Your real name? Then my assumption was incorrect; you're not a professional.'

'Open the door?'

'Never.'

I grasped the pistol with both hands, lowered it till it pointed directly at his crotch. 'Open the door,' I repeated.

'Well, perhaps it is a little stuffy in here. He turned and complied with my request. A cool breeze filled the compartment.

'Now, Herr von Seydlitz,' said I, my eyes, over the pistol sight, locked on his. 'On the count of three, I'm going to pull the trigger. Between now and then, of course, you are free to do as you will. One . . . two . . .'

He was suddenly gone. I stood, raced to the door. Leaning out, I could see him sprawled facedown on a pile of boulders below the embankment. I threw the pistol out the door, then closed it. Retrieving the Suez shares from the floor, I resumed my seat. I stared blankly at the floor.

Would I have shot on the count of three? I tried to concentrate on the question. It seemed important. But it was no use.

Dear Miss Everleigh:
In case you think otherwise, I am happy to inform you

that, except for a few minor burns, we are all alive and well. It was my intrepid son Noel who saved the day. At the time in question, he was resting after some strenuous activity on behalf of the lovely Miss Deborah MacDill. It seemed as if the floor caught fire simultaneously in four or five places. It took but a moment for us to realize that we were trapped behind locked doors. Under such circumstances, the only resource is to panic and have done with it. But miraculously an escape route materialized — an opening in the wall!

Noel, of course, had simply unlatched an opening into one of his secret passageways. Before that, I knew nothing of his world between the walls of Fanshawe House. (But he has since informed me that you did and of how you came by the knowledge.) I must say that at the time, it came as a most pleasant surprise. All of us — ladies first, of course — scrambled through with no trouble and we soon found ourselves, miraculously, in the pantry, where, along with the servants, we evacuated in good order. I decided on the spot that under the circumstances I would refrain from disciplining Noel for keeping the whole thing secret for so long.

As for the rest of it, I too have friends in high places (though not so high or respectable as yours). They inform me that a certain Heinrich Werner von Seydlitz Holstein, a minor prince of some sort, was found dead near the railway embankment a few miles from Doncaster. The Suez shares were not on his person. Poor fellow. Was he pushed or did he fall?

That leaves just one possibility, in which case congratulations are in order. For a beginner, you did marvellously well.

Life is, after all, only a game. I can only say that since I lost this particular scrum, I'm pleased that it was not to a foreigner. You are, as am I, one of Britain's own and it is best to keep this sort of thing in the family. God save the Queen and all that.

And be assured, dear Jenny, that I will certainly win the next scrum.

Fanshawe House, though it suffered badly, will be back on its feet eventually. Miraculously, the old wing that we had sealed off managed to escape undamaged. We are, for the time being, living in it. In two years or so, however, when the renovations have been completed, you are invited to return, not as an editor (my memoirs are ashes, unfortunately) but as an honoured and most beautiful guest.

I've been told to pass on to you the admonition from my wife that you must practise the exercises she taught you and you are to eat an adequate amount of carrots and fruits and nuts, but not too much else.

Allow me to say in closing that it's not whether one wins or loses that counts, but rather how one plays the game. You and I played it well. 'Twas that other fellow who was such a rotter.

Good health, my dear. And regards to my old friend Edward. God bless him too.

> Yours,
> Sir Harry

P.S. Under separate cover, you will find a bit of salvage.

There was a small box. Within it was my ruby necklace. The gold had melted somewhat into a grotesque shape. I vowed never to have the stones reset.

Before its return, Edward gave me a beautiful and extremely precious diamond necklace to replace it. Though my appreciation is profound, the ruby necklace, despite its twisted flaws, remains closer to my heart and I will always wear it more often than any other. It is, after all, a glowing testament to a most gracious adversary.